BLOODLETTING GO

e. m. roy

For Sully

chapter one

WHEN DECEMBER FINALLY CAME AROUND, Joel had been waiting for at least thirteen hair-graying minutes in the coffeeshop booth. He made sure to blame this fact on her dedication to the intricate craft of latte-serving, and not the line of waiting patrons leading from the counter through the open doorway. More than one of them gave him sideways looks and sighs. "I better see some passion in that foam art," he said as she approached.

December untied her apron before she slumped down across from him. "You're a dickhead." She placed the latte he'd ordered on the table between them with a clatter. Customers murmured near the entrance to the cafe and someone shouted off in the distant kitchen.

Joel looked up and down the line of customers. "Should you be, uh, taking a break right now?"

December followed his gaze, then shrugged. "Either I sit here and do nothing for ten minutes or I murder the next person who orders an oat milk latte. Take your pick."

He looked down into his mug with newfound discomfort and wrapped both hands around it. December smirked.

His best friend usually toned down her style while on a shift at Cracked Kettle, as the mandatory beige canvas apron was a bit of an aesthetic-killer, but today, she worked around it. When she untied the apron and shoved it into the corner of their booth with a scrunch of her nose, a black band tee with an illegible chicken-scratch font and a weird skeleton creature printed across her chest was revealed. Joel suspected she'd get told off again if Mandy caught her wearing that on duty. That, and the clunky silver rings on almost every long finger probably made serving coffee in ceramic mugs a noisy endeavor. Her blonde hair was unkempt as always, short on the sides and halfheartedly styled up in an overgrown faux-hawk that crawled over her ears. She rubbed at her eyes, pinched the bridge of her nose as if to soothe a headache. Then she froze, eyes still closed. "Can I help you with something, Coleridge?" She looked up at him with a squint. "Why're you staring at me?"

Joel shrugged. "I just think it's funny, Des."

"What's that?"

"That you work here at all. Mandy's crew isn't exactly…"

"I *know*, man."

They watched the other baristas serving out drinks for a moment, most of them looking, well, not like December.

Long hair up in ponytails, or subtly patterned button-down shirts secured up to the collar. The type that resembled history or philosophy students. Joel had studied English (which was very, very different than those, he would argue) and barely got his bachelor's with his life, relying heavily on his companion for help with literary analysis; Des herself had studied education, of all things. And here they were. Unemployed, and working at Cracked Kettle, respectively.

One brunette barista shot them a stern glare, earning a stifled giggle from Joel and a narrow-eyed smirk from December. The barista's face turned inexplicably red and she scampered behind the counter. The customers in line grumbled.

He looked back and forth between Des and the back room where the barista had disappeared. Noted the thickness of the air as Des cleared her throat in amusement. He'd been around Des long enough to know what that meant. "So, what, you're just in everyone's pants around here?" Joel said, gesturing with his head in the direction of the avoidant barista, and taking a sip of his still-too-hot latte.

"Oh, bite me. Not the guys."

"No duh."

"What about you? Markus worked here for a while. Clearly you're not immune to the allure of miserable waitstaff."

"I have no idea what you're talking about." This being one of the most fly cafes in Portland, his asshole ex had of course had a brief stint as one of Mandy's minions. He was more than happy to never see Markus working in Cracked Kettle again. Or in general.

Joel scanned the rest of the staff lazily. He paused, then cleared his throat. "So, what's the plan for tonight, Des?"

A goofy grin lit up her face and Joel couldn't help but smile in return.

She gestured theatrically, "Oh, *debauchery*, of course. Some band is playing tonight at Redacted down the street. I say we head over there."

Joel grimaced. The last time he and Des went out to the club on a Friday night, it had ended with him very nearly getting punched in an alley, and her breaking a finger on the face of the drunk douchebag who'd gone after him. The bruises on Des's knuckles were pretty badass, but the ones on Joel's ego were still sore.

Cracking her fingers one by one, Des eyed some of the increasingly impatient customers shuffling in wait for overpriced coffee. "Come on, dude. It'll be fun! Maybe there'll be some idiots there to terrorize with our radical progressive ideology."

It wasn't that she hated her hometown, per se. By all accounts, Portland was pretty accepting. The bookstores she frequented downtown, for example, were warm and cozy, towering dusty novels feeling like home even in the harshest of Maine winters. There were quite a few havens that didn't care who you were fucking or what was in your pants. It was the people, she surmised. People ruined places. Turned buildings into bigots and homes into hives.

Joel rested his chin on his hand, leaning on the wooden table. His tone was drawn out with equal parts disdain and adoration. "December Paige, you are a menace to society."

She took that as a yes. Flashed a wolfish grin and leaned back in triumph. "A lavender menace," she corrected, "And I take great pride in being such, baby boy."

His mouth opened in indignation, but before Joel could come up with a sharp retort, a small figure hovered over to the pair's booth. The girl had pastel pink dyed hair with short bangs, a flowy cream crop top and ripped denim jeans that hung low on her hips. She was cute. And exactly Des's type. Joel watched as his friend's demeanor shifted, as Des adjusted her shoulders and considered the girl.

However, the girl was looking at him. "Hi, there," she said. "You wouldn't happen to be Joel Coleridge, would you?"

"I am," he said. He shot Des a questioning look, and she shrugged.

"I'm Laurel. Laurel Sweetser." She glanced between Des and Joel quickly, then offered a smile that scrunched up her eyes more than it should have. "Markus's girlfriend," she clarified.

Joel choked on his latte, sputtering into the crook of his arm until his face turned bright red.

Des tried her best to hold in a thunderous laugh. Her feet kicked under the booth in giddiness.

"Oh!" he exclaimed once he'd contained himself. "Um. Hello. Joel," he extended a hand.

Laurel took it, and shook his hand lightly, seemingly unfazed by their reactions. "A pleasure! Markus told me lots about you. I'm kinda new to Portland: just moved up here from Amherst not too long ago. So, you must be December? I've heard about you, too." She turned her attention to Des and looked her up and down under hooded eyelids.

"I guess I must be," she said.

"You have such an interesting name!" said Laurel.

Des set her jaw. Whatever initial interest Des had shown in Laurel evaporated from her face with that single comment.

"So, listen, Markus and I are going out to this super underground club tonight. I think it's called Redacted? It's supposed to be all the rage. You two should join us!"

Des began, "We actually had plans—"

"We're down," Joel said at the same time. He'd be lying if he said he wasn't curious to see Markus with this new girlfriend of his. Laurel seemed much too nice for him.

A stern glare shot his way from Des, and he tilted his head quizzically.

Laurel paid the exchange no mind. "Sweet! Here's my number. I can call you tonight with the details. This'll be so fun; Markus will be so happy to see you." With this last remark, she trailed a featherlight hand down Joel's arm in a gesture that could have been either friendly or flirtatious but left goosebumps in its wake all the same. Des tracked the movement.

"Cool, uh, we'll see you guys then," he said.

"Coolio." Laurel left their booth with a small wave as quietly as she arrived.

Joel watched her pastel pink head disappear through the front door of Cracked Kettle, weaving between waiting patrons. He nearly jumped out of his skin when he turned to see Des scowling over at him. "What?"

"Something's off," she said.

"I know. There's no way Markus found someone that nice."

"No. I mean… Laurel just seems like—"

"*DECEMBER!*" A horrendous voice boomed from the kitchen, startling them both.

"Shit," Des muttered as she stood up to hastily tie back her apron just as Mandy the owner stormed out from behind the counter of the cafe.

Des hurried over to the cash register before the woman could scold the loitering distraction named Joel. He bit his cheek to hold back his laughter.

chapter two

DES COULDN'T STAND BEING AROUND anybody—even Joel—whenever she had things to process. There was no way she would be able to talk to him about Laurel, anyway. How Laurel'd sized her up in her periphery more than once. How in her mind's eye Laurel hovered between Markus and Joel like a magnet orbiting two poles. Tethering them together for her own amusement, it seemed, and basking in the orchestrated tension. That, or Laurel was terribly unaware of her surroundings. Des supposed either was possible.

She needed the sort of quietude unique only to bookstores and libraries, where she could zone out and wander amongst the aisles without looking over her shoulder. The weight of written words on all sides provided a boundary, a forcefield between her thoughts and her body, where she could allow the fictional problems of others occupy the space in her head instead of whatever asshole-of-the-week she and Joel had come across. It was peaceful and fuzzy. The bookstore in question was void of life save for Des and some movement in the back from an unseen worker.

It was dim in the afternoon light and a couple of lightbulbs overhead must have burnt out. Volumes overflowed from mismatched shelves to stack in precarious towers on the floor. A few step-stools lay scattered about the tight aisles so folks could reach the uppermost books.

Des sat down on one, low to the floor. The smell of old paper, ink, and dust were all comforting things. This was one of the only bookstores she'd found with a dedicated, extensive horror section, just left of the sci-fi and fantasy aisle. She combed the rows of books and was pleased to find they'd been reorganized since she was last here. There were familiar favorites; *The Shining*, accompanied by a thorough Stephen King selection; some beautiful editions of Clive Barker's *Books of Blood*; a Shirley Jackson trio with *The Haunting of Hill House*, *Hangsaman*, and *We Have Always Lived in the Castle*. Des felt her posture relax. She trailed a finger along the spine of this last book.

She thought, not for the first time, about how she would have loved to share the works of Shirley Jackson and others with students. That was the sole reasoning behind her degree in education. Des wanted to talk about literature, analyze it, and give students the space to learn more about themselves in the process of doing so. The distance of fiction allowed self-exploration in a way no other medium could. So, she'd gotten her degree. And tens of thousands of dollars in debt, a shitty Portland apartment with Joel (whom she'd had to lead through his own English degree), and a job at Cracked Kettle when none of the local schools were hiring.

Looking up, now, she felt very small. Sitting on the step-stool made the bookshelves loom above her, touching the ceiling. She felt like a child without the innocence or ignorance of youth. She knew the system was rigged against her and yet she still allowed herself to become victim to it, hoping against hope that something might change for the better. That she could talk about books with students who cared and not live paycheck to paycheck, not skip meals so that she could pay off her loans, not have to spend her twenties making overpriced coffees for Portland's artsy-metro-elite with their matching plaid skirts and blazers or collared polos with the tips of their slick hair bleached almost white. She tucked a stray strand behind her ear.

Her toil was a raw edge. But it was her own. It was real. She found that in that moment it wasn't a bad feeling. Nor was it good; it simply was. For once she allowed herself the space to fold and sit in surrender under towers of stories she would never have the time to read.

Feeling small was only unbearable when other people made her feel that way, she diagnosed. When they misconstrued her work at the coffee shop with a lack of ambition or disinterest.

So instead she commanded the room. Diverted people's attention to herself or elsewhere with a few well-chosen words or gestures. Controlled the narrative. She'd show that she worked intentionally and unapologetically. No customer-service voice or banal platitudes. Even if that meant pissing off a few customers. And her boss, despite doing her actual job very well. Joel seemed to deeply respect this about her as it was a power he had never really possessed.

But then Laurel met them at Cracked Kettle and put Joel under a spell. She didn't trust the pink-haired girl. There was something calculated in the way she spoke to them. Purposely getting under Joel's skin, and looking down at Des with a shrewd stare.

Maybe Joel truly didn't see it.

Des, on the other hand, was waiting for the other shoe to drop. But what was she after? It seemed like she wanted to get close to Joel, but why, when she was dating his ex? It's not like she could do anything about it without knowing why.

"Oh!" The bookstore worker flinched behind an armful of novels when she saw Des sitting on the stool in the horror aisle, just a pace or two from tripping over her. Des nearly jumped out of her skin.

She was about Des's age, auburn-brown hair tucked into a ponytail, and wide greenish eyes peering over the stack of books she was carrying. The topmost volume teetered and fell unceremoniously with a thud.

Des picked up the book from the floor. *American Psycho*, Bret Easton Ellis. The volume was hefty and worn in her hands: a pre-owned edition. "You dropped something," she mumbled, teasing in an attempt to reclaim the encounter.

"Sorry," the worker said. "Didn't realize there was anyone else here." She bent down carefully and set the stack of books on the floor, shaking out the ache in her arms as she straightened. "Mind if I join you?"

Des's skin prickled. She did mind. But the worker was familiar, she realized; she'd chatted with her a couple of times in passing when she visited the bookstore. Couldn't remember a name, though, which surprised her, as she was incredibly attractive. She blinked. "Sure," she said. Her face got hot. "I mean, no. No, I don't mind." The heat in her cheeks was unbearably foreign. She felt the need to run away and hide. The worker had caught her in a moment of vulnerability that Des couldn't shake off.

The girl's mouth twitched at the corner. "Evelien Holmes," she presented. She bent to retrieve *American Psycho* from Des's grasp, suddenly at eye-level.

Des tried to ignore the way their fingers brushed as she did so. Freckles and acne scars dotted her face, eyes creased in the outer corners from an oft-worn smile not currently sported to its full capacity. Des had trouble making eye contact.

"December Paige."

"Nice to meet ya." Evelien placed the book on the shelf before them, shifting a few others to make room for it. She towered over Des. The novels in the stack Evelien had carried over began their meticulous placement onto the horror shelves, the bookstore worker careful in their organization.

Des shifted on the stool, trying not to gaze up at her with what she feared were wide, wondrous eyes.

It was odd, being in this position. With other girls, Des was more than comfortable showing off her confidence. It's what she'd always done. Attracted girls with a dominant persona she pretended wasn't worn like a mask. She could even fool herself with the façade. Something about Evelien threw her off, though. What it was exactly, she couldn't pinpoint. It was like she flipped a switch in her brain. Perhaps the softness in her belly, the spindly fingers so perfectly suited to page-turning, the swell of her thighs which Des could secretly admire from her current angle—

"So, what brings you to sulk so sweetly in the horror section today, December?"

Her mouth went dry and she fiddled with her lip ring. "Nothing in particular," she said.

"Looks like you have a lot on your mind for someone just loitering."

Des let out a breathy chuckle and shook her head.

"Girl trouble?" Evelien said. Des considered her carefully before deciding how to respond. Noted a silver ring on her thumb, and smirked.

"Not mine, surprisingly," she answered.

"Well, now I'm even more intrigued."

She scratched at the nape of her neck. Here was this familiar stranger, somehow compelling Des's thoughts from her tongue with ease. "It's incredibly boring," she shrugged. "Just that my best friend, Joel—his ex, Markus, is seeing this new girl. She's cute and seems nice enough. We met her at my work this morning. Cracked Kettle," she answered before Evelien could ask. "This girl—Laurel—it's like she's…too nice. Overcompensating, maybe? It's hard to explain. Joel and I are going out with them tonight and it's gonna be impossible to avoid any drama in the first place. But I can't read this chick at all, and the night has the potential to go sour really quick."

"Huh." Evelien considered this as she continued reshelving books from her stack. "Is there any chance this Laurel girl genuinely is a decent person, and you're being overcautious for Joel's sake?"

"No," she said. A pause. "Yeah, probably."

Evelien giggled. It was a lovely sound. "Well, December, I think you sound like a really good friend who's concerned about someone you love getting hurt again. Use tonight to observe them. Don't give anyone an ultimatum, because that's not fair, but watch and see how Joel reacts to his ex and this new girl being together. Give her the benefit of the doubt. And if things don't go well, you can just remove yourselves from the situation. Who cares, right?" The bookseller leaned over Des and slid a volume between two others on the shelf just above her head where she sat on the stool. She smelled of vanilla and old paper, a late autumn day.

In all honesty, Des cared. She cared a lot. Redacted was their place; removing themselves from it over a squabble with Joel's ex felt like a lame betrayal. Giving up a place where they could safely be who they were meant to be over a little bit of stupid romantic tension. If anything, Markus and Laurel should be the ones to leave. Together, the pair passed as straight. They did not need the brick walls of Redacted's humid basement bar to feel comfortable in their identities or to publicly enjoy their relationship. Des wouldn't let them push her and Joel out of there. She would need to come up with another plan to get rid of them if it came to that.

Maybe Evelien's suggestion wasn't a bad idea. Give her some time to think of a worthy punishment for the newcomer and the ex.

She would wait it out and see what Laurel's true intentions were. Better to sit back and watch, let Laurel pretend that she was the one in control for a while and see what she would do. Watch Laurel dig her own grave, by Des's design. She just hoped no one got hurt in the process.

Des rose to her feet. Evelien was an inch or two taller than her. She cleared her throat and hoped she wasn't blushing. From the look on Evelien's face, though, something certainly gave her away. Fuck it. She lowered her eyelids in a sultry gaze. "What do you say you join me tonight and we can keep an eye on them together? You seem pretty good at reading people, Evelien Holmes."

She smirked at that, taking her bottom lip between her teeth. "Where are you all going, exactly?"

"Redacted. Just down off of Congress Street."

"I know it. The punk bar."

Des searched Evelien for any sign of unease. When she came up empty, she raised an eyebrow in a dare. "I'll see you there at nine?"

"You might," Evelien said. She looked Des up and down, causing her skin to crawl. "If I didn't know better, I'd think you were using this problem of yours as an excuse to invite me out and get me drunk."

"You don't have to drink if you don't want to."

"And they say chivalry's dead." Evelien's grin widened as she turned and walked to the back of the bookstore. "Perhaps I'll see you later, December. For now, get out of my shop, I have to close up."

Des laughed, had to resist the urge to skip out of the store like a moonstruck schoolgirl. She reached up and traced the outline of her smile with her hands. This was going to be fun.

chapter three

GRIME, GRIT, MOSHING BODIES, FLASHING lights, the smell of skunk and stickiness of spilled beer—December was in her element.

The local band on the waist-high stage at Redacted's basement bar was alright, mostly playing covers of crowd-pleaser punk jams that always garnered elated screams of recognition from the pit below within the first few chords. Crypt Collapse was the band's name, written in blocky duct tape letters on one of the amps. It wasn't so much about the band itself, though live music was more than welcome.

Des bounced in time with the music, the sweaty bodies of strangers all around her doing the same. Everyone yelling along to each song unable to hear their own words over the cacophony. Shoulder to shoulder. She panted, felt herself shoved to the side, caught her balance on a bystander and pushed back into the crowd with all her might. Des loved dancing in the pit. As much as you could call it dancing.

An unlucky young man fell to the floor as the pit surged in front of him, his dangling chains clanging. Des shouldered someone else out of the way and held out a hand to him in the darkness, which he took gratefully before anyone could accidentally step on him. His mouth moved in what might've been a quick thank-you before he disappeared again and Des resumed moshing.

She had lost track of Joel a couple of songs ago. Redacted was their usual haunt, but granted it wasn't often this lively, so she didn't blame him for standing back and enjoying the show from the sidelines. The first thing she'd taught him when they started coming here was the forearm signal, for his own safety: a single raised arm across your chest and parallel to the floor meant you weren't there for moshing and folks would leave you alone. "Do people actually try to punch you? Like, in the face?" Joel had asked, eyes a little wide as he mimed the gesture.

"No, it's not about being violent. We're just having fun. The big shots who come in throwing kicks and punches are dicks who will get thrown out. No one likes that guy. You just have to dance, help people up if they fall, don't be an asshole," she'd explained. "Moshpit etiquette is a thing. I'll educate you." With a devilish smirk, she'd done just that and made Redacted a near-weekly hangout for the pair. Although, Joel preferred the more casual crowds that came about whenever there wasn't a live band playing, and it was a mainstay that they both always had the most fun when they were able to claim a booth in the back corner of the bar, far away from the stage, to share some drinks and laughs.

Tonight wasn't one of those nights.

A bead of sweat dripped down Des's spine as the bass rumbled through her chest and made her ears ring. Her feet were sore, and a bruise would likely form on her shoulder by the morning, but she felt alive.

It was hard to make out any faces in the darkness of Redacted's basement. The bodies around Des were anonymous organisms, here to push and shove and scream, a universal release of primal energy. Caught in intermittent flashes of colored light. Pinks and blues and reds. A faceless crowd like a singular organ that throbbed in rhythm and ecstasy.

The song ended, and Des breathed heavily, hands on her head. In the brief pause, voices in the pit around her bubbled to the surface, all shouting over one another and in the absence of the music.

Someone gripped her shoulder. She whipped around and steeled herself in case it was some random trying to cop a feel.

"December!" a high-pitched voice cut through the noise. Between the ambient lights she was met with Laurel Sweetser. She was in a short denim-blue dress that showed off her cleavage and hugged her bony hips, complete with dangling earrings (which shot Des through with anxiety like an arrow, being in the middle of the pit where they could easily be ripped clean off) and lots of rosy blush across her cheeks and the tip of her nose. She looked like a cartoony, pastel doll. The trendy look rather suited her. Fake and all for show.

Laurel smiled at Des, but was glancing side to side nervously. "We were looking for you! I think, ah—" She stumbled into Des as the crowd nudged her from behind. "Come get a drink with us!" Closer now, Des could feel her breath on her skin.

She leaned away. "Is Joel with you?"

"And Markus!"

Well. Better go save her roommate from his ex, then. She allowed Laurel to take her by the hand and lead the way to the outskirts of the pit, teetering a little along the way as she wove between the moving bodies.

They finally reached the bump in the floor that ran through the middle of the basement where the black-flecked concert flooring met fake hardwood. Warm lighting and the bar itself appeared. Des scanned the weekend bar-goers—more of them than usual—in search of Joel.

People bustled about and spoke up over the noise, a lot more subdued at this end of the establishment. Redacted drew a crowd made up of mostly younger punks, with a handful of veteran metalheads who had nowhere else to go that played halfway decent music here in Portland.

It was easy for Des to picture herself and Joel becoming the grumpy old queers who still frequented the spot even if their tattoos were faded and their hair was gray. The kids would recognize them, get up to let them sit at their favorite booth. They'd scare off the idiots in the pit who were being obnoxious or violent. Discuss the new Misfits compilation album, talk about social ethics with a new generation of riot grrrls and other feminist punks. It was an earnest image. A lovely one.

A pair of the older, more grizzled men at the bar eyed Laurel up and down as they passed. Des removed her hand from Laurel's and instead placed it around her shoulders, staring daggers. Even Laurel didn't deserve to be checked out by drunk creeps. Not here, not in Redacted. The idea made her blood boil.

Laurel blinked.

Plus, there was the added malicious joy of getting a reaction out of those two idiots.

One of the men snickered, shaking his head, while the other set his drink down on the bar with a clank. He was dressed up more than his fellow patrons, in a light work shirt and tie as if he'd just left the office. Quite out of place on its own. On closer inspection, though, the shirt was wrinkled, tie slightly askew, and a couple days' worth of stubble shaded the lower half of his face. He looked tired. A bit ill. Taken advantage of by the day job. Des wasn't sure what he'd do in his current state. She hurried Laurel along.

When Des glanced over her shoulder, the man was still glowering down at them from the bar.

As the music faded down with each step, Des spotted a disgruntled Joel sitting in the booth furthest from the dance floor. His eyes widened as she approached, an unmistakable help me.

Des bit down a grin.

Markus, looking similarly uncomfortable across from him, nodded a 'hello' that Des mirrored.

Laurel grabbed Des's hand again and pulled her close to the booth. "Look who I found!" she presented Des with a flourish.

Des lifted her eyebrows. "Been a while, Markus. How're things?"

Markus opened his mouth to reply, but Laurel cut him off. "Things are great! I'm so excited we could all get together. This place is so…" She looked around.

The older men who had eyed them as they passed were still staring in their direction. Laurel didn't seem to notice; or, if she did, she didn't care. The fine hairs on the back of Des's neck prickled. "Grunge!" Laurel decided.

Markus snickered. It was a wolfish, toothy expression that she recognized from so many months ago when he and Joel had been together. "Sure is," he said. "Come sit down, guys. Hey, remember last time we were here, Joel and I got so drunk that Des had to basically carry us home?" He nudged Laurel as she slid down into the booth beside him, while Des sat stiffly next to Joel.

Her companion seemed fixated on picking at his cuticles.

Des cleared her throat. "The last time *you* were here, you mean."

Markus's grin faltered. "Uh, yeah," he said. That was the thing with people like Markus; and Laurel, for that matter. If they were not present, if they were not participating, the place did not exist. The world only existed as far as their eyes could see. Beyond the door, nothing. Void. If a tree fell in the forest, it only made a sound if Markus and Laurel were there to hear it. Society was immaterial beyond the limitations of their experience. Which was the only experience that mattered, after all.

"So how long have you guys been together?" Joel asked. The question was directed to Laurel and did its best to disregard Markus completely.

"Few weeks!"

"A couple of months!"

Markus and Laurel answered simultaneously. The latter giggled, leaning into Markus's shoulder. Des signaled to the bartender that she and Joel would each like a shot of something strong, please.

It was past nine o'clock at this point. Des wondered if Evelien would show up at all. It didn't matter; she didn't care. She could hook up with some other stranger instead once all the Laurel business was taken care of. The thought stung.

Several minutes of half-hearted attempts at small talk ensued, during which Des and Joel downed two shots of tequila each while Markus nursed a beer and Laurel sipped a colorful cocktail. She bobbed her head to the music, a gentle swaying against the violent thrashing of the live band playing at the far end of the bar.

Des was just about to make an ass out of herself by asking Laurel if she recognized the song that was currently playing—obviously she wouldn't know it—when she felt a hand on her shoulder, long fingers gripping bare collarbone.

Evelien had changed her clothes since Des had seen her earlier that evening. The cozy burnt orange cardigan had been replaced by a cropped black and white striped vest with matching low-rise pants. She was stunning.

"You're late, you know," Des said.

Joel simply watched, half-buzzed, sensing where the night was about to head.

"Sorry. Had some work to get done." Before Des could ask what duties a bookseller could have outside business hours, Evelien extended a hand to her friend in the booth. "You must be Joel," she said.

"I must be," Joel echoed Des's response to Laurel from earlier that day. His smile was despondent, but he shook her hand anyway.

"This is Evelien," Des introduced. "That's Markus—and Laurel," she gestured to the other two sitting across the booth. Evelien nodded knowingly as Laurel launched into exclamations about just how fresh-and-trendy-and-bold her outfit was. Something about color-blocking that Des would have been more interested in had she been sober.

"Nice button," Evelien said with a grin. "Very subtle." The one she'd indicated on Des's jacket read: *I am a member of an immoral subculture.* She kept her hand on her shoulder.

"Well, subtlety's the name of the game." She tilted her head up at her, dangerously close. She tried to focus on the real reason she'd invited Evelien. To help her keep an eye on Laurel. Right.

Joel cleared his throat. "So—" He swirled his drink. "Laurel. Speaking of subtlety. Are you flagging?"

Markus choked on his beer, but Laurel looked confused.

"The handkerchief," Joel clarified. "Hanky code." It was folded neatly in the front chest pocket of Laurel's denim dress like a pocket square. Not proper hanky code etiquette, Des was about to point out. Usually if you were flagging it would go in the back pocket of your jeans. Left side for dominants, right side for submissives. While flagging wasn't as popular among the queer community here in Maine, the practice was still recognizable. There were so many colors with different meanings these days. Each one indicating a different sexual preference. It was impossible to keep up with. By the time a new hanky code trend trickled its way up here from Boston, it was old news that no one bothered explaining. She rarely wore handkerchiefs herself as a result for fear of being misunderstood.

"Oh!" She smiled. "Not intentionally! What does this one mean?" Her handkerchief was yellow.

"Stop it, Joel," Markus sputtered. Des felt like she was watching a car accident about to happen. What did yellow mean, again?

"What? It's cute, just a pop of color. Would actually go nicely with Evelien's outfit!"

"Joel—" Des warned.

"It means you like piss." He buried his smirk in the drink.

Laurel's face went bright red.

But Des stood up before anyone could speak. She was fighting for her life trying not to burst with a full-belly laugh. Distraction, need a distraction. Escape? Escape sounds good.

"Dope, well, we're gonna go to the bathroom, be right back." She grabbed Evelien's hand and disappeared into the crowd, disregarding the rest of the table's glares.

chapter four

DES LED EVELIEN'S SILHOUETTE DOWN a short set of rickety stairs and into the bathroom. The chains on her belt clamored as they went, in contrast to the other woman's soft footfalls. The music, once deafening, dulled, the sound making its slow, syrupy way through the walls and growing quieter by the inch, the vibration of the bass becoming a low roar.

The bathroom was small and shabby. Paint chipped off the door, while taped flyers advertising local shows, cute and not-so-cute political stickers, and Sharpied writing covered every flat surface, including the smudged mirror above a little sink. It smelled of bleach and weed. The door shut behind them with a slam that would've been more startling had their ears not been ringing from walking through the pit.

Slightly drunk, Des leaned on the sink before the mirror. She met her own glassy eyes as a dazed smile crept over her face. She put her hand up to touch it and confirm it was real. Real, if delirious, after having to sit there and cringe through everything said so far tonight. She hoped Joel wouldn't be too upset with her for leaving him out there. It might be good for him, after all.

A laugh erupted from her lips. "Do you think—who pisses on who?" She wheezed, almost doubled over. "Is Laurel a *pisser* or the *pissee?* HA!"

"I think Joel is poking the bear," Evelien said with just a smirk.

Des caught her breath. "Maybe he should."

"You like causing trouble, don't you?"

Evelien stepped up behind her. Close. Placed her hands on Des's hips and pressed them together. Des didn't move, but caught her eye in the mirror. Evelien tilted her head, a wordless question with a merciless gaze.

Des found herself blushing and needed to look away.

The girl behind her laughed, then, and wrapped her arms more fully around Des's waist. It was secure, safe. "You sure talk a big game for someone this nervous around me."

Des almost flinched. "I'm not nervous. I'm just… This is usually…the other way around," she said, feeling small in her grasp. Every inch of her back was touched by Evelien's body, curve for curve, fitting together perfectly.

"Ah, I see." Evelien's hand wandered up from her waist, grazing her chest until fingertips traced her collarbone. Mapping out the structure there and watching them in the mirror as she went.

Des's face reddened. And then an agonizingly light touch to her neck, her windpipe framed by Evelien's delicate hand. When she swallowed, the touch made her feel like she was burning alive.

"Well, is this arrangement okay with you, December?"

She nodded to the mirror with glazed eyes. All thoughts of the three individuals waiting for them outside in the booth vanished.

Evelien tightened her grip by barely a degree, just enough that she would be able to feel her racing pulse. "Words, please."

Her lips parted and Des could barely recognize for own flushed form in the mirror, held firm yet careful. "Yeah. Yeah, it's okay," she whispered.

Evelien smiled with a hum, rewarding her with a peck on the cheek. They swayed slightly, whether from the alcohol or from the muffled music seeping through the walls of the bathroom, she wasn't sure. "This is ridiculous," Evelien said into her back after several moments. "We're in here while chaos reigns out there. Too bad I won't be able to help and sort it out because *somebody's* being far too troublesome. Stealing me away like that." Her lips brushed Des's neck, and Des let her head fall back on her shoulder.

Right, yes, the reason they were here. "What do you— uh, think of Laurel?"

"I think that Joel has a lot of conflicting feelings," she countered. She met Des's eyes again in the mirror, serious.

"Do you want to leave? Get him out of here?" Evelien traced circles on her collarbone, leaving sparks in her wake.

In fact, leaving Redacted was the last thing Des wanted to do right now. In answer, she pushed back to grind against Evelien.

She exhaled into her bleached hair. "What am I gonna do with you?" Evelien murmured.

This prompted a giggle. Des liked the look of them together; her own dazed expression complementing Evelien's mischievous, darkened brown eyes peering out from behind her. It was a new and dangerously indulgent sensation. "God. I should *not* have invited you out," Des said.

"Oh yeah? Why's that?" Her breath was hot down Des's neck.

"You're gonna kill me."

Evelien turned her around so they were face-to-face, and pinned her against the sink with her hips. The change in perspective was overwhelming. "Maybe I am." She pressed her mouth to Des's, who parted her lips hungrily, and unbuttoned Des's jeans.

Joel willed Des to feel the frustration he bore into her back as she melted into the crowd with her date. The air was thick around the remaining club-goers in their booth.

Eventually, Markus gulped down the rest of his beer and set the empty glass on the table with a clink. He wiped his mouth with his fingers, brushing the stubbly facial hair there. Joel remembered what it was like to kiss him when he hadn't shaved. Bristled and savory. He shook his head.

"December seems like she's doing pretty well for herself," Markus said.

Laurel's hand snaked over to interlace with his.

Joel shrugged. "The usual."

"She still working at Cracked Kettle? She always made the best cappuccinos while I worked there. The only thing good in that shithole, especially with Demanding Mandy running the show."

"She's still slingin' coffee, yeah. She's actually really good at it."

Laurel piped up, beaming at Markus. "I can just imagine you working there and making this one a coffee." She nodded across the table. "Sorta like *Dream for an Insomniac.* So damn romantic."

"Well, we didn't exactly quote philosophers back and forth. Not sure who would be Jennifer Aniston in this situation." Joel tucked his hands into his sleeves.

"I am *so* glad you got that reference." Her finger danced around the rim of her cocktail glass.

"No, I think either of us would need to actually read for that to happen," Markus laughed.

"I read sometimes." He'd been a damn English major. His ex forgot?

"Sure, you do." Laurel winked at him. She pecked Markus's temple. "You two together must have been adorable. December must've simply died."

In his half-drunk state, Joel reminisced. He thought they'd made a handsome couple. They were both a bit stockier, though Markus was taller, built like a high school football player. Not the stereotypical gay relationship dynamic, where one of them was expected to lean more femme. Both men were rough-hewn and comfortable in their queerness. And Joel liked that. It was different than what he was used to, an added layer of exhilaration beyond his previous flings with women, though he'd enjoyed those as well. Ultimately Markus had broken it off, simply citing a desire to see other people, and not much reasoning beyond that. Joel suspected (and December had diagnosed) that he'd been spooked by the seriousness of their relationship and wasn't ready for a long-term partner. Possibly a fair fear to have. Joel still thought it was bullshit, though.

They'd broken up around the same time Markus had quit his job at Cracked Kettle in favor of some corporate managerial role; Accounts Supervisor and Data Entry Specialist of Sales and Projects and Blah Blah Blah I Want To Kill Myself Manager, if he remembered correctly. A most prestigious title.

Joel cleared his throat, studying his ex, who busied himself by people-watching the other bar patrons and clearly pretending not to hear Laurel's commentary.

Distantly he wondered what the hell Laurel did for a job. Or maybe she was a trust fund kid. Now that he thought about it, she had Daddy's money written all over her. Must be why Markus liked her so much; he didn't have to think about their shared bills or rent or groceries, didn't worry at all about the role she played on this earth, didn't wake up every morning with ennui plaguing her like fluid in her lungs. She didn't bleed like he did. That's for damn sure.

Or, alternatively, he might just be drunk right now.

The girl in question was looking up at him through her eyelashes as she took a sip of her drink. She smacked her lips together and set down the glass, then gave Markus a slight nudge. He seemed startled when she spoke again. "Listen, Joely. We have a proposal for you."

"Oh? What's that?" A sinking feeling settled in the pit of his stomach.

Markus stammered. "I mean, you don't have to say yes, it's totally cool—"

She shushed him. "Markus and I were just wondering. It might be fun to mix things up a bit." Laurel reached across the booth and ever-so-gently brushed his knuckles.

He ignored the shiver down his spine.

"Would you have any interest in having a little *ménage à trois?*" Her French accent was atrocious.

A threesome? Was she serious? Joel would be lying if he said he wasn't at least somewhat interested. But his indignity got the better of him this time; he wouldn't let himself sink down to that level. The several drinks in his system almost cried in protest of the refusal. He snatched his hand away from Laurel and stood. "Very funny," he grumbled. On an impulse, he grabbed Laurel's fruity drink and downed the last couple of ounces, much to Markus's mortification.

The glass clattered as he set it back in front of her—she didn't break eye contact. "It's a serious offer," she said, too calm. "Don't you think it would be fun?"

Markus whispered something in her ear, but she didn't acknowledge him. He couldn't meet Joel's eyes. Coward.

"Fuck you guys." Joel got up and disappeared into the pit.

He wished Des would make him a coffee.

chapter five

DEAFENING. RINGING IN HIS EARS. Vibrations through his ribcage, down through the soles of his shoes, into the floor. Eardrums popping. A burgeoning headache that would be infinitely worse tomorrow. Claustrophobic in his own skull. Joel needed to do something.

What would Des do if her dignity had been insulted like that? She'd start a fight, probably.

Away from Des, away from Markus and Laurel, he pushed through the crowd of moshers until he was in the midst of a group to the side of the stage where the band was covering some rough, growly song he had heard before but didn't know the name of. This group of people was having a good time—flailing their arms and jumping all around. Joel set his sights on a taller man with spiked-up black hair. On a different night, he might've thought this guy was cute. But not now. He ran between two other people with all the rage in the world and rammed his shoulder into the back of the man, knocking the wind out of both of them and sending the unsuspecting guy to the ground.

The crowd split around them as the guy stood up, clutching his wrist.

Joel put his fists up and the other man grinned.

People around them backed away as much as they could. Not much, in other words.

The taller man swung at Joel and caught him in the side of the jaw.

Joel could no longer hear the music. Absorbing the punch with hardly an acknowledgement, he went for his opponent's nose, and felt it crunch under his knuckles.

"AHG! Dude, what the fuck?" The spiky-haired man held his face as blood dripped from his nostrils. "Thought we were having fun here."

"I'm not having fun," Joel said, a red bruise already forming on his jawbone.

"Asshole." He grabbed a fistful of Joel's shirt, pulled him in close, and landed a sucker-punch right under his left eye.

Joel fell backwards in a heap. The pit closed in around him and someone stepped on his fingers. Tears streaked down his face from an eye that was already swelling. He kneeled, turned around, but couldn't see the guy he was fighting anymore. When he tried to take a deep breath, it came out as a sob.

He'd been punched before, obviously. Something was different about this one. He tentatively touched his cheekbone and winced. Some sort of shape was indented into his skin where the guy's fist had connected; the spot was raised in an unnatural way, skin split unevenly. He must have been wearing a ring. Joel's fingertips came away bloody.

Laurel's proposition. Markus's shame. Des's abandonment. He wanted to curl up on the beer-soaked floor and lie there, bodies shuffling all around him in an inscrutable rhythm, sometimes kicking or stepping on him, until he was worn away to nothing and became just a bloodstain on the black linoleum.

A hand grasped his shoulder then, and he looked up.

December searched his face, kneeling down to his level and holding his chin with a light touch to get a better look at his swelling eye and cheek. Her skin was flushed and strands of her blonde hair stuck to her temples, concern knitting lines into her forehead.

Joel swayed, dizzy. Des might've said something then, but Joel couldn't make any sense of it, as she put his arm around her shoulders and pulled him up to his feet, gripping his waist with her other hand. She guided him out of the pit and down the rickety stairs of Redacted into the bathroom.

If he closed his eyes, which was easier to do with his left one swelling up by the second, he could almost pretend he was in their apartment. Warm, dim, walls busy with art and postcards and sticky notes and photos. They could barely afford the shitty little one-bedroom in Portland. Des slept on the pull-out couch mattress in the space designated as their living room while Joel had the small bedroom. It probably should have been the other way around given how many girls Des had brought back home over the couple years they lived there. But Des had insisted he have the bedroom, and Joel had been surprisingly spared of innumerable awkward encounters by some stretch of luck, so the arrangement worked for them. The radiator creaked and groaned in the winter nights and all the door hinges had been painted over with chipping white paint from a decade ago. It smelled of Des's cologne, coffee from her job at Cracked Kettle, and Joel's sporty deodorant. A collage of mismatched decoration and furniture, some of which they'd found for free on the side of the road. A coalescence of lost things that somehow found a home together.

The slam of the bathroom door jolted him out of his reverie. Stickers and colorful graffiti littered the brick walls. Joel's reflection in the mirror was startling; the skin under his eye was red, turning purple. He stepped closer and leaned on the sink. The indentation from the man's ring stuck out vividly, the skin cut and bleeding. Beneath the clotting blood he could just make out the shape of a pentagram.

"Kinda metal, if you ask me," Des said, running a paper towel under cold water. She gently wiped the blood from his cheek.

Joel let out a sad chuckle, leaning on the counter. He shook his head.

"You wanna tell me why you went and picked a fight with that guy?"

He did his best to stifle the heat rising in his face, mostly because it hurt to scowl. "Not really."

"Well, too bad. Tell me." She threw the bloody paper towel in the sink and folded her arms, looking down at him.

"Fucking Markus and Laurel, that's why."

Des's face softened. "Baby, you can't—"

"Stop it. Don't do that."

"I'm just *saying*, you can't let Markus's latest fling get to you. You know it won't last. And you could do so much better than him, anyway. Dude's a townie."

"It *does* get to me, and there's nothing I can do about it. It's not even that he's seeing someone. It's that it's *her*." He ran a hand through his hair and tugged on it.

She tilted her head a bit then but chose her words slowly. "What do you think about Laurel?"

"There's something about her. Like she's…getting off on us being together before. I don't like it."

Des's eyebrows raised. "Yeah." She sighed, rubbed the back of her neck. Let's take a page out of Evelien's book. "Maybe she's just trying to be supportive? In an ignorant way?"

"She asked me to have a threesome with them."

There goes that. Her lips parted. "Shit."

Joel threw his hands up. "I hate her, I hate them both, and I don't know what to do—"

Suddenly the bathroom door busted open. They both jumped, and Joel yelped.

Laurel's pink pigtails shone under the overhead light, Markus close in tow and Evelien following a few steps behind.

Des froze, eyes wide. Had she heard them?

Laurel's face was flushed, hackles raised. "Are you fucking serious?" she snapped. Des took that as a 'yes.'

Markus removed his wrist from her grasp with some difficulty. "Hey, hey, it's fine, he's just misunderstanding…" His tone was tight and he shot Joel a glance.

Evelien hovered by the bathroom door and fiddled with the hem of her vest.

"I don't think he is, actually," Des said. A muscle jumped in her jaw. She steeled herself to argue on Joel's behalf.

"*Stop* it, Des!" Joel shouted.

She blinked in confusion. He didn't want her to fight for him? Why the hell not? It's what she'd always done.

Before she could respond, Joel turned to Laurel. "And *you* need to get the fuck out of here. This is our place, not yours. We're not here for you, we are not your kind, we're not just some fetish!" The pentagram mark on his cheek was bleeding again, a drop falling down his face like a tear that stung the broken skin.

Laurel straightened, took a step forward, and pushed him. "I don't know what you're talking about," she said.

The drop of blood from his cheek hit the floor with the push. A pinprick of vibrant red. Joel righted himself quickly and got up in her face. "You do. You're a degenerate disguising yourself as an ally—"

"Oh, I'm the degenerate? You fa—"

And then, the world held its breath. Something shifted in the atmosphere, as if in some dream, some horrible reality, and Des caught her own eye in the mirror as her reflection began to blur like it was in motion.

The room was moving.

Tremors through the floor. But more than the music outside could ever muster. The mirror clattered against the bathroom wall until a crack split their image into a million shards. A great clamoring, the whole building above them trembling, feet on an unsteady ground unable to gain traction.

"What the fuck?!" Laurel shrieked.

"Earthquake," Evelien said, and as she seemed to register the fact, with more urgency: "It's an earthquake!"

Des leaned her back against the wall to stay upright. The vibrations ran from the concrete wall up her spine, into her skull. The lights flickered, the hanging fixture swinging back and forth and casting the bathroom into a rapidly warping shift of shadow. She caught a glimpse of Evelien crouched like a cornered animal by the door.

Markus held tight to the paper towel dispenser, which buckled under his weight with the relentless quake, and sent him tumbling to the floor with a shout.

Joel, arms splayed in the far corner, stayed upright.

Laurel must have locked herself in the stall. She was screaming.

Des had heard stories about earthquakes before—saw them from the safe distance that her parents' old, static-filled CRT television covering world news provided. They happened in faraway places that Des would probably never see with her own eyes. California. Japan.

They didn't happen in New England, much less Maine. Their buildings were probably not made to withstand such shaking weight. They could have minutes before Redacted collapsed on top of them, pinning them down in the depths of a forgotten gathering place where no one would ever find their remains.

Wrong wrong wrong. Something was very wrong.

The light fixture swung dizzyingly above as the foundation shook and shook. Des choked down panic, tried to find a single point in the bathroom to focus on, to help regain her balance. Her eyes refused to concentrate in the tumultuous mayhem. She closed them, and the darkness was far worse.

Instead, she found Joel's wide, terrified gaze. His tears watered down the blood on his cheek and ran down his neck. He opened his mouth and might have been calling her name as the mirror shattered on the floor beside her.

They seemed to stay in that moment for hours, years—the bathroom of Redacted an unrecognizable haze, Des and Joel on opposite ends, struggling to be each other's sole anchor in a world that heaved to rid itself of them like poison in its stomach.

Bricks shook out of the wall and clattered to the ground in a choking swirl of dust. Water erupted from the toilet and flowed under the stall along the floor in erratic streams. Des's senses were in overdrive. A roaring crescendo. Her throat tore loose a scream. And then—

Silence.

The grumbling ground faded off into a dead stillness. Nobody dared to move. Her heartbeat throttled in her ears, the only other sound besides the slowly squeaking light hanging from the ceiling, performing its last residual swings from the violent momentum of the moments before. The swinging light and the debris around them were the only evidence that something had happened. Something had changed.

Several beats passed. "I-is everyone okay?" Joel's voice trembled from his corner. He was still bracing himself against the wall, dust coating his hair.

A sob came from the closed stall, and Laurel burst out, running full speed into Markus, who struggled to keep them both upright and looked as if he might vomit.

"I think so," Evelien said softly, holding out her arms for balance as she stood up at a snail's pace. "December? All right?"

"All right." She tried brushing off the dust from her clothes, kicked the shards of broken mirror off to the side. It was no use trying to create any sense of order in the bathroom now.

"Then let's get the fuck out of here." Evelien trotted on unsteady legs to the door and shoved it open with her shoulder, while the other four followed briskly after her.

chapter six

DES EXPECTED GIANT CRACKS TO fracture across the floor of Redacted like in an apocalyptic movie; people scrambling for purchase along jagged cliffs, climbing out of a void in the ground, splintering wood and shattered foundation, club-goers either running around in a blind panic or tending to the wounded. Half of the concert floor pushed several feet away by broken earth below, endless cracks down into darkness. She expected dust in the air making it hard to breathe. Or the building partially collapsed on top of them, sealing all of Redacted's dedicated moshers and bar crawlers in a dingy tomb under Portland. A continuation of the pandemonium—first that of the pit itself, and then of the earthquake, and now of the aftermath, people still bustling about and stumbling over each other to get to the exit upstairs. She expected more of the sensory overload she had grown accustomed to, not just of that night, but of the general overwhelm of her existence up until that point.

Whatever she expected to see upon emerging from the bathroom, it was not this.

Evelien led them up the small set of stairs to the main basement floor of Redacted. The concert floor and stage to the right, the bar and booths to the left, as always. But Markus and Laurel paused suddenly. Des bumped into them, colored lights cresting over their heads. "What? What is it?" She pushed forward to get a better look and braced herself for the carnage.

But there was nothing.

The club was completely empty.

There were no cracks along the floor, no crushed bodies, no debris. No people running to escape the earthquake. Redacted's space was spotless. No one sitting at the bar or in booths, no pit, no live band. Not even any trash, nor evidence to prove that these things so integral to the place had ever existed before.

And it was dead silent. Not a single other person in sight.

After an eternity, Markus spoke first. "Did they all… get out somehow?" he asked. His fingers twiddled with a belt loop in the waist of Laurel's dress, who didn't seem to notice.

Evelien opened her mouth to speak, but no noise came out. She cleared her throat and stepped forward onto the dance floor. Vacant, dead, unblemished by the crowd it drew. She put her hands in her hair, mindlessly tying it in a messy knot as a nervous tic. "Um, no. Hold on. Just let me think about this."

"Des?" Joel's hand gripped her arm and she realized she had wandered out of the mini corridor towards the skeletal bar, dreamlike. He was almost hyperventilating.

"It's okay," she heard herself say. "It's fine. Let's just get out of here." She watched the five of them as if from afar, detached from her body. Following Des across the floor. It seemed more vast than it ever had been before; an ocean of nothingness, dotted with pink and blue lights that continued their eternal swirling dance despite the lack of music and bodies to touch. They reached the stairs the led up to the exit, also unaffected by the earthquake. A metal staircase not unlike a fire escape crawled up to a short brick hall, illuminated only by the red EXIT sign above the industrial door at its end.

When the group got to the top of the stairs, urgency finally won out. Des broke into an almost-run, lunging for the door handle. Everyone else was tight on her heels. Heart pounding. She turned the handle.

It didn't budge.

She blinked. Tried again. Not even the click of a latch. Her stomach dropped. Pressed down harder on the handle. Pushed her shoulder against the cold metal. "Come on!" Panic. Soon she was throwing her entire body weight at it, again and again until she was sore. "Fuck, shit!" *Bang, bang.* The door would not open.

Markus shoved her out of the way, Des's back scraping brick. "No way," he said. Washed in red light from the exit sign. He kicked the door. It took no pity, not even courtesy enough to creak. Kicked again, this time directly on the handle, trying to break it.

"Stop! Stop!" Laurel was crying, the first words she'd been able to speak since leaving the bathroom.

"You'll trap us in here if you snap off the handle," Joel said, pacing.

"We're already trapped!" Markus yelled. His face was florid and scrunched.

"Just hold on, hold on, let me think," Evelien repeated.

Everyone had a desperate turn to try their luck at the door. It opened for no one and didn't give the slightest indication that it would ever move again. "Oh my god, what the fuck," Markus breathed, eventually sliding down to sit on the floor, back leaning against the door. Laurel joined him there.

The five of them were stuck in Redacted, alone, cut off from the world.

Des couldn't look at Joel. She knew she'd see her own fear reflected back at her. She scratched at the inner side of her arm. The earthquake did something—something was very, very wrong.

It would be one thing if they were trapped down here with everyone else in Redacted. The moshers, the men sitting at the bar, folks on the sidelines and in booths, even the band that was playing. Crypt Collapse, they'd called themselves. But Redacted was as barren as she'd ever seen it. Crypt collapse… The building could not have fallen into a new fissure in the earth; there'd be rubble, destruction. Bodies. But could it have collapsed another way? Through some other, unseen dimension?

No. That would be crazy.

A few moments of quiet passed as everyone caught their breath. "A phone," Evelien said. "They must have a phone here." She took off back down the stairs without waiting for a response and they all scrambled to follow.

The air was heavy with the absence of Redacted's usual commotion. Des felt lost being on the empty concert floor, crossing the shell of the bar and being able to hear their footsteps as they went. Evelien pushed past the small swinging doors between countertops to get behind the bar, looking high and low, jostling glasses aside. On the far wall she finally found the landline. She picked it up, a payphone-style metal wire connecting the phone to its box, and put it to her ear, punching in 9-1-1.

They waited. And waited. Evelien grunted and pressed down the switchhook a few exasperated times before putting in the number again.

Joel wrung his hands.

Nobody dared to speak.

Dread pooled in the pit of Des's stomach.

Colored lights filtered over Evelien's face in dazed, oblong circles as she typed in 9-1-1 for a third time, holding back tears. "The line is dead," she said in a broken voice, still holding the phone to her ear. "Not even a fucking dial tone."

At last Laurel lost it, and sobbed.

Joel paled and looked as if he may faint, bracing himself against the bar with white knuckles.

"What is this? What the fuck is this?" Markus asked no one.

"Give me the phone." Though it was futile; the only thing Des could hear through the landline was the echo of her own blood rushing through her ears, like listening to the ocean through a seashell. She slammed it back onto the hook, rattling its box on the wall. And with the force, the wire detached, hanging lifeless and swinging from the plastic phone.

They all stared with wide, terrified eyes. The phone wire was frayed at the end and dangling accusingly. "You broke it?!" Markus grabbed Des's shoulders and shoved until she lurched against the bar, clattering glasses. "You just killed us!"

"I didn't do anything! I didn't break the goddamn phone!" She stomped on his foot and Markus stumbled. No way in hell she would let him take out his frustration on her.

"Fuck off, it's not her fault." Joel pushed Markus back, putting himself between them.

"You stay out of it. This bitch just cut us off from our only way out of here," he was pointing at Des, who scowled, eyebrow piercing pulled taut. Sobs and sniffles continued from Laurel, sitting slumped in a stool. Des planted her feet and got ready to throw a punch.

Evelien knelt, inspecting the wire. "No, Des didn't do anything," she said. They froze in their argument as she held it up, smaller wires poking out of their long metal casing. Makeup smudged, hair in a wild knot at the crown of her head and dust from the bathroom covering her clothes. Her expression was grave. "The wire was cut. A long time ago, it looks like. It was barely attached to the wall."

That was it, then.

Des crumpled to the floor. Anger evaporated from her body. Helpless in a place that was once familiar and safe but now prompted only a sense of dissociated terror. They were all going to die here.

chapter seven

"I'D BE 'BEWITCHED, BOTHERED, AND bewildered,'" Des said.

"Okay, well, no duh. But what would you *do*? Get creative." Biting his nails and asking random hypotheticals offered Joel little distraction from the situation at hand, but he tried his best to give Des some lighthearted entertainment. This particular question: *How would you survive in the apocalypse?*

Maybe their definition of lighthearted entertainment could use some work.

She gave some thought to it. How would December Paige get by at the end of the world? Currently, she was splayed out over four barstools, head dangling with her bleach-blonde hair falling undone in a short mane. She watched as Evelien sat alone at a booth, the upside-down angle making her look as though she were hanging from the ceiling like a resting bat. Evelien kicked off her heels and buried her head in her hands.

"I'd 'drink before the war,'" Des said. As Joel's confused scowl came back into focus, she clarified with exasperation, "I would stick with you. And Evelien. Until 'the last day of our acquaintance.'"

"That could come sooner than we thought, depending on how long we're trapped down here." Joel touched his cheek gingerly, wincing with his good eye. "Why're you talking like that?"

She narrowed her eyes. "'How insensitive.'"

"Come on. This feels weird, doesn't it?" The dancing lights felt like ennui in motion; no moshers to bathe in blues and pinks, nothing to break their hypnotic cycles. Without bodies to catch the movement of the colors, the lights' patterns were repetitive against the clean swath of Redacted's floor. Forming listless oblongs without direction that mindlessly retraced their steps. "This place is —was—like our home." Now, staying another moment trapped in the club felt like suffocating.

"'Success has made a failure of our home.'" Des couldn't stifle a smirk this time.

He whipped around then. "Wait. You're just quoting Sinéad O'Connor songs at me. We get it, Des, 'nothing compares 2 U.' Irish lovin' dweeb. Were you even listening to anything I said?"

"Yes, yes, I was." Des let her arms hang over her head off the stool. She lowered her voice. "It is weird. But you asked how I would survive in the apocalypse. I'd keep going, like we have been tonight."

"You saying this is the apocalypse? With the earthquake and everything?" Joel picked at his cut, prompting a bead of fresh blood to peek through his cheek.

Des scoffed. "No. That'd be wack." She swatted his hand away from his face.

Pacing a distance away, Laurel busied herself with combing the outer edges of the establishment. She looked like a caged animal. Des could only assume that she was trying to find some other way out, which was pointless. They were sealed away below street level. She thought about telling her to stop, but decided it would only spark more problems between them. Instead, she watched as she touched several bricks in the wall to test for looseness.

"So, what, you really think someone's just gonna show up and get us out of here?" Markus spat, evidently listening in. "Have you looked around at all? This isn't normal. Where the hell did everyone *go?*" This last word turned into a shout that reverberated off of Redacted's windowless walls. It wasn't clear exactly who he was talking to.

"They must have been evacuated during the earthquake, that's the only explanation. So, the bartenders or whoever will find us when they open up tomorrow. We just have to wait," Joel said. The desperate twinge in his voice let Des know he didn't believe these words himself.

Markus threw his arms up, but it was Evelien who spoke from her seat across the room. "They wouldn't have just abandoned the place. And the register looks like it's closed out, there's no trash anywhere, no empty glasses. It's been cleaned. There's no way there would have been time to get everyone out of here and close up shop while we were in that bathroom. The earthquake didn't last that long. It's impossible." She grabbed a fistful of her own hair.

Des knew Evelien was right. Her head spun to make sense of it, but couldn't comprehend the sequence of events. Earthquake. Which, first of all, never happened in Maine. Or, they did, but they were very rare. Hiding in the bathroom, away from a crowd that was likely panicking. Coming out of the bathroom—to a completely empty, almost sterile club. Something was missing. It gave her a headache. Or maybe that was just the blood rushing to her head.

Colorful lights swirled around the floor to a musical beat that no longer sounded from the dead speakers. Des felt both within and without. As if the five of them had been plucked from the reality of that night, and deposited onto an empty set. Where no actors remained to carry out their respective scripts but the bones of some familiar theatre persisted. The curtain stuck open. A derealized space with the eeriness of a play that has not yet begun.

"Maybe it wasn't an earthquake," Laurel said in a small voice.

The statement struck Des. If it wasn't an earthquake—

"What else could it have been?" Joel bristled.

"Why do you have to talk to her like that, man?" Markus stepped up, inches away.

But she wondered. What else could it have been?

It was strange, that was certain. The rarity of an earthquake in Maine, first of all, and then the disappearance of all the other bar-goers. The lack of commotion and the eerie silence. It was almost paranormal. "What if there's something supernatural happening here?" she mused.

Both Joel and Markus whipped around in matching scowls.

Her bloodstream boiled. "Do any of you have a better explanation?"

"I'm trying to think, I just need to think," Evelien said. The boys returned to their heated conversation.

Des grumbled and watched the upside-down argument, her head still dangling off the barstool. Considered what Joel might look like if Markus gave him a black eye on top of the other one he had already received that evening, underlined with its pentagram-shaped cut in his cheek. The two of them puffed their chests and shouted, Markus just a bit taller. Laurel looked on with glassy eyes while Evelien seemed not to notice the commotion from her booth. Perhaps Joel's accusation was true; Laurel was transfixed by them, breathing each other's resentful breaths, flushed. This was not what Joel and Markus's relationship had been like in its prime, but that didn't seem to matter now. The sound of two men arguing was ingrained in women throughout the history of civilization like a tornado siren. Seek shelter immediately. Even Des felt it, she was loathe to admit—an intrinsic tension in her muscles from their barked obscenities. Markus grabbed Joel's shirt collar and Laurel gasped. She played with a strand of hair as they fought. Eating up the danger of it. Sadomasochism entwined with internalized bigotry was a dangerous combination.

Alright. The stools creaked beneath her as Des sat upright, warding off a dizzy spell from the movement. "Enough—" she began.

Evelien screamed.

The light shifted beyond Markus and Joel, a silhouette in the dim that darted across the floor with running footfalls. Frantic and fast, the steps grew louder, and then melted into the wall, indiscernible from the other shadows.

Oh, fuck.

Des jostled off of the barstools and toppled two of them over in her haste. They both banged against the ground, making Laurel shriek. Pure flight instinct took over. Laurel scrambled to the safety of the warm-toned light of the bar where Evelien remained, hugging herself. Des dove into the booth opposite her.

"There's someone else here," Evelien said, breathing heavy as Markus and Joel hurried to join the girls, argument forgotten. Joel was pale as he clambered into a creaking seat next to Des.

"Did you see it?" Markus asked in a hushed voice, crouched in an adjacent booth.

"Just a shadow of a person. . . ."

"I heard someone running."

"Shit—"

A small flicker of hope felt like a shot down her throat and it was impossible not to latch onto the rush it gave her. "Hey!" Des called to the other side of Redacted. "We know you're there!"

Joel hit her arm, and the others stared.

"What? It must be someone else trapped from the earthquake. Maybe they know what's going on." The possibility of getting answers was too alluring. Also, fuck this guy for scaring them at a time like this. For scaring Evelien. She wasn't about to feed into it, that's for sure.

Evelien's eyes were wide. "I don't know if we should—"

Footsteps sounded from across the concert floor, an irregular and neurotic beat. *Thud-thud-thud-thud,* running closer and expertly avoiding the colored spotlights that were still writhing along. Then the thing paused, just a few steps before the steady light from the bar would be able to crest their outline.

Everyone shrank in their booths. Des's heart pounded. So the person-shaped shadow was not a friend. Noted. She met Markus's eyes; sweat beaded his brow. He nodded in the direction of the intruder, gestured between them. Exhaled through her teeth. Des assented and they stood.

"Are you fucking stupid?" Joel shout-whispered. "What are you doing?"

"They could help find a way out of here," Markus said. Des signaled that it was okay, she had it under control.

Better to move than sit and wait to die, anyway. She would be the one to go. Punch some information out of this guy if it came to down it.

Joel folded into himself as she left the booths.

The odd pair of Markus and Des tread forward, everyone else staring daggers into their backs. They neared the outer reaches of the bar's light, where the concert floor began. No shape materialized from the shadows. No more footsteps. Markus gazed at Des, who raised her eyebrows. Gave him the go-ahead to speak. He cleared his throat. "Hello?" Silence. "Hey, me and my friends got stuck here during the earthquake. Do you know a way out?"

She considered the possibilities here: a bartender, or a customer, who had been hiding like them and was now terrified of the unexplainable circumstances. Maybe one of the creepy men at the bar, here to hit on Laurel or call Des a dyke now that they couldn't escape. Or someone— something—snuck in during the commotion.

They waited.

"You're kinda freaking us out, man," Markus continued. "Can you just come out where we can see you?" He strained to make out anything in the dark.

Several beats passed until the hairs on the back of Des's neck rose. The disquiet was suffocating now. She took a half-step back while Markus passed the edge of the darkness. Time to regroup. She opened her mouth to call him back and—

A voice crackled with phlegm and malice. *"We're closed."*

Two beads of red reflected in the shadows and blinked. A squelch before either could speak.

Markus shuddered. There was an outpouring sound of liquid spattering the floor.

Des couldn't move.

Running footsteps scurried away into the dark, a wet chewing noise accompanying them. Murkiness spread at Markus's feet.

"What was that?" Evelien called from far behind them.

With absolute dread slowing her hand, Des touched Markus's shoulder.

He turned, and there was a gaping hole in his chest, blood gushing out. The second time this evening that blood had been spilled onto the Redacted floor. Strings of sinew streamed from his sternum. Des could see his splintering ribs jutting out on either side, just make out the column of a spine further back. Wet lungs palpitated and blood flooded from the wound. A gaping void between the organs.

His heart was missing.

Markus fell in a choking, twitching heap.

Des scrambled backwards, tripping over her feet, her horrified wail alerting the rest of the gang. "What the fuck, what the fuck—"

Upon reaching them, Laurel howled and grasped at Markus's body. A steady stream of red coated her hands and the floor. His face was slack, jaw hanging in a silent scream and eyes rolled back to their whites.

Evelien and Joel appeared at each of Des's shoulders where she sat on the ground. "Oh my god," Evelien said.

"What happened?" Joel's voice quaked.

Des realized she was crying. "There was a voice…" He helped her to her feet and they stumbled back to lean on the bar. She struggled to articulate the red pinpricks in the dark, like a deer's reflected eyes. How Markus's chest had moved as if he was pushed and pulled. The savage, moist noise as the shadowed creature had snatched the beating organ and slurped into it.

"You didn't even do anything! You just *watched!*" Laurel cried, holding his face. "Please, someone help him!" For the first time, Des felt powerless.

Evelien had cautiously gotten closer and peered at the gruesome scene, the gory hole in Markus's sternum. "Is… Where's his heart?" she gagged. "Did that thing rip it out?" She scanned the club for signs of movement, to no avail. It was gone.

Joel's gaze was stuck to the floor where Markus's body lie. A body he once knew so well, now without the organ that gave him life. His heart consumed and flesh still. Too still. The remaining alcohol in his stomach churned. He trailed the edge of the bar, one hand skimming its wooden surface.

The urge to distract Joel from his former partner came over Des. Spare him any ounce of this pain. It was no use, she knew. What she could do was make sure that shadowed creature didn't come back for seconds. She took a deep breath, wiped her stinging eyes, and started to tell them to get away from the widened pool of blood soaking into well-worn flooring.

A deep and muffled sound echoed from outside the club before she had the chance. Joel wrenched his attention from the body to Des, amber eyes wide.

"Guys—" he said, and the colored lights flickered as the ground began to rumble, "it's happening again."

chapter eight

THIS EARTHQUAKE WAS WORSE THAN the first they had endured. An amplified aftershock? Something else? At least the bathroom had provided some false pretense of shelter. Now they were exposed, in the wide-open bar and concert space of Redacted, and vulnerable as the ground convulsed beneath their feet.

"Get under the bar!" Des shouted over the bedlam, grabbing Joel's arm and pulling them both to crouch between stools under the small overhang. Glasses shattered around them, falling off shelves to hit the countertops and the floor below. Evelien dove beside them, as Laurel hastened to hide under a booth.

Markus's limp body shuddered in its pool of blood mere feet away. Ripples spread across its thick, tacky surface. He lay in the barren center of the dance floor, nothing to shield his body from the quake.

A wave of dizziness threatened to drown Des, whether from motion sickness, fear, or disgust, she could not discern.

The earthquake spread the blood in an uneven, slushing array across Redacted's concert floor. It glistened under the chaotic listing of strobe lights and caused strange shapes to take form in the gore. The body swayed. Droplets jumped up with the inertia, rolled out from the pool, fleeing. One splatter like a blinking eye. A distorted, demonic face whose red-black irises melted across the floor and threatened to caress Des's feet. The corpse became a Rorschach test of blood splatter.

And then the ground opened up with a sound like crushing bone, and Markus's heartless body sloughed into a jagged void. His blood followed in rivulets down the hole and was consumed by the earth.

Laurel may have been screaming several booths away.

Joel gripped Des's forearm with bruising force.

Evelien sat hugging herself with her head on her knees.

The four of them waited for years, or for seconds, until the quaking ground gradually turned still.

The roaring died away, and the colored dance lights had ceased, leaving only a soft white glow behind the bar. The concert floor and the stairs to the bathroom were imbued in gloom. Des's breathing was loud in her ears. "—Are you guys okay?"

A bead of sweat ran down Joel's his temple and cut through the dust plastered there. He nodded wordlessly.

Two earthquakes in one night. Perhaps her supernatural supposition was closer to the truth than she'd thought.

A figure walked into the dimness from the far side of the bar. Des blinked as her eyes adjusted, steeled herself for a second heart-eating shadow, and instead saw Laurel gazing into the depths of a massive crevasse in Redacted's floor. The crack went across the concert flooring and into the hardwood of the bar space, leaving splintered boards like daggers along its edges.

Markus's body was gone, his pool of blood faded and cut down the middle. It was different, though. The blood looked old. Could almost be mistaken for spilled brownish paint. Completely dry, stained into the flooring as if it had been shed decades ago. A lifetime ago. Nothing resembling the wet gore soaking the room before the earthquake.

"What is that?" Evelien pointed to the wall across from the bar where they crouched.

The brick wall was crumbling in several places, exposing dusty wood beams, insulation, and sheetrock behind it. Withered. An earthquake of this magnitude would have damaged the infrastructure in some way, surely, but this was a far cry from that. Not sheer force had caused this damage. It looked as though time itself had.

The dilapidation was not what Evelien gestured to, though; there was a wider stretch of the wall where the bricks remained intact. Words were spray-painted across them in dried, dripping red, newer than the aged blood on the floor but not at all fresh.

WE ARE IN HELL.

Were they?

"That wasn't there before," Laurel said in a broken voice from the other side of the cliff. Her words bounced off the edges and faded into the empty depths.

The whole of Redacted was changed. Primeval. Sat abandoned for decades while dirt and debris accumulated inside and the foundations rotted. A forgotten space left to decay.

With them trapped inside it.

The graffiti Evelien indicated wasn't the only of its kind, though it was the biggest and most prominent, even overlapping some other hurried words in places. Tags in various spray paint colors and handwritings were scattered along the broken brick. *Die fag* appeared more than once; a swastika that had been sloppily painted over but retraced; *Dykes are good for 1 thing!*; *plague rats*; *commie scum*. The longer Des looked, the more words she made out in the dim lighting.

There were also a few numbers painted sloppily in some corners. *1995.* The current year muddied in what used to be white spraypaint.

2001, below that in faded blue.

2013. Dripping, dried pink.

2027. A brighter yellow spray overlaying the others. Next to more slurs in the same color.

They were still in Redacted, but in some alternate future where the business had gone under, building sat uninhabited for at least a generation, then was claimed by the horrific antithesis of what it had originally stood for.

Des ran over to the corner of the bar and vomited.

Redacted was desecrated.

The place stank of hatred and rot. Perhaps for the first time that evening, Des felt unadulterated terror seep through her bone marrow. This was horribly wrong. A setting which offered them respite now riddled with disease and pollution. It was an abandoned beehive dried up and flaking and ready to be torched; its inhabitants were long dead, and only the outsiders who viewed them as pests remained, eager to burn the shell of the nest so that their comrades could never feel safe here again. How insidious a thing, to go looking for yourself in a place you used to belong, only to find a wasteland of corruption born to spite your very existence. To erase you from your own history.

Bile mixed with alcohol stung her throat something wicked and she retched until nothing was left in her stomach, leaning against the wall. When she felt a hand on her back, she flinched, but didn't turn.

"I don't know what's going on…" Joel said, "but we're gonna get out of here. Okay? We'll find a way out, I promise, Des."

She collapsed back under the bar and looked at her friend. The cut on Joel's cheek was swollen and angry, blood scabbing over the now-illegible pentagram. His eye was barely open.

"This is Redacted. We're still here, just—Fuck, I sound insane," Des managed between breaths. "Look at this place. It's old. Vandalized. In a way that hasn't happened yet."

The red graffiti across the way lured his eye. *Hell.* "2027," he read. "...I don't understand. Are we being punished?" Joel asked.

"I don't know," Des said.

It was particularly cruel—splitting the establishment right down the middle, cold and exposed in pre-winter air. Scars and whispers were the only evidence of the communities it had once been home to. Anything and everything was tainted. Redacted was a violated husk and December felt much the same.

A cynical part of her recognized the irony. How *this* dirt and grime was not *her* dirt and grime. The bold words on the walls spat in her face. In any other situation, that may have made a compelling idea for a zine; "good" vandalism versus "bad." She'd made a small handful of do-it-yourself little pamphlets before. One particularly embarrassing one from a few years back filled with poetry she'd written inspired by Shirley Jackson. Joel had loved it and still kept a copy on his scuffed bookshelf. A thinly-threaded-together collection of photocopied scrap papers bound by orange cardstock. There'd also been more timely zines. She was no artist, but she had words. Called out political inaction on the AIDS crisis, xeroxed riot grrrl messaging. Pinned them to an old corkboard near Redacted's bathroom until the papers inevitably were discarded or swiped by interested onlookers. There was even a time she'd hidden a couple of copies in the booths at Cracked Kettle just to get a reaction. Her boss Mandy hadn't been happy about that. Cheap, inconsistent, messy, unprofessional, at times distasteful and venomous. Beautiful. Especially when she came across zines by her more artistically gifted peers. There was nothing on earth quite like a homegrown anarcho-punk book of quiet rage or screeching reverie making the rounds through all the local queer folk. Whispered references to writings that sometimes came with no author attached, a spontaneous generation of musings. Often tough to track down more copies once the original batch had been distributed. The result was ephemeral collections of handwritten, or typed, or screenprinted hyper-niche ruminations born out of grunge, where a single page could knock you on your ass and send you spiraling with tears down your cheeks or acid in your throat.

She wondered if she would ever see the outside of this alternate-Redacted and find another zine again. Funny how the little things are grieved the most.

Joel was searching her face, concern and despair pulling his brows together. He said something she didn't hear and sounded a mile away. A slow, shaky breath rattled in her lungs. "What?"

He wiped his good eye with a shirtsleeve. "I'm sorry. I'm so sorry."

"You have nothing to apologize for."

"I know, but—I'm just sorry. Des…I'm going to get us home. Whatever it takes. We'll go home to our apartment and I'll make you breakfast and this will all be a bad dream."

Des couldn't hold back a snicker, but her heart warmed all the same. "Joel Coleridge, cooking breakfast? You set off the fire alarm making toast last week."

He coughed on a laugh. "Okay, maybe I'll leave breakfast to you. I just know we'll need something good to nurse this inevitable hangover. An oat milk latte, preferably. None of that instant shit. The good kind that you make." Marginally less tense now, Joel lowered himself to fully sit under the bar next to Des, their shoulders brushing.

Her eyes went wide then, stomach dropped to the floor. "You know what? I was supposed to open at Cracked Kettle tomorrow. Or today, depending on what time it is." Absurd guilt surged through her gut. She needed this job. Rent was due next week. Or thirty years ago, if she believed the graffiti. Hah. "Think I could call out?"

Joel was quiet, then bubbled up in a giggle he tried to suppress. "Dude. Mandy's just gonna have to deal with it. We're kinda stuck in a basement that's been the epicenter of multiple earthquakes in one night. These things come up, man, can't exactly request the day off in advance."

Des tsked. She hated the part of herself that instinctively worried about work and bills when their friend was dead and they were trapped in an interdimensional nightclub, so she made herself sit in the painful absurdity of it. The rest of the room came back into focus.

On the other side of the crack in the floor where Evelien must have jumped across, she stood gazing at the graffiti several paces away. Laurel gazed into the abyss.

"Markus," Laurel's voice cracked. "His blood looks so— old?" She knelt to touch the brown stain.

Blood. From Joel's pentagram-shaped wound to the murder of Markus, so much had been spilled on the floor of Redacted tonight. And right after those two occurrences, both earthquakes hit the building. It could be a coincidence, but…

"And how did all of this even get here?" Laurel's voice carried through the room as she turned to take in the graffiti. She craned her neck to see the full expanse of spray paint and chalk.

"I don't know." Evelien walked cautiously along the wall.

"Maybe we just didn't notice it before?"

"I would have fucking noticed Nazi graffiti in any bar I went to."

"Well, maybe you just *didn't*, smartass bitch!"

Evelien ignored the outburst. "It's like the earthquakes…brought us here, somehow."

"But we're still in Redacted," Joel interjected from beside Des under the bar. "We never left."

"Yes, but *when?*" Evelien was pacing now. Even from a distance, Des could see her trembling.

"When what?" Laurel snapped.

Des shot a worried glance at Joel. Evelien sounded crazy saying it out loud for the whole group to hear, but wasn't that the same conclusion she'd reached? "We're still in Redacted," Des confirmed with hesitation, glancing between the group, "but at another point in time. I think. An alternate future. Or, *our* future. Look at how the place has aged. Like it went out of business and was abandoned. Even Markus's blood looks older. Almost ancient. First it was Joel's cut, and then Markus… Both times they were hurt, their blood touched the floor. What if blood caused the earthquakes? And the earthquakes transported us to this other-Redacted?"

Evelien stared at Des and slowly nodded.

"Fuck." Joel ran his hands through his curls compulsively.

A quietness settled over them as they considered this. Dark swaths caked the hem of Laurel's dress, draping stiffly over her legs. The chafing feeling of dried blood on denim…Des winced. "You're all delusional," Laurel said.

"If you have a better explanation, Laurel, I'm all ears," Des said. The other girl was silent.

Evelien wrung her hands and did a half-step before freezing, as if she were resisting the urge to pace again. "Okay, right. An alternate dimension. Triggered by blood. Great. That's fine." She rubbed at her brow and took a deep breath. "If the building has changed, or aged,"

Evelien began, "We should try the exit again. Maybe the door's changed, too. It could be unlocked."

Checking the exit for a second time was as good an idea as any. Joel helped Des to her feet and they crossed the crevasse with great care to join the other two. Averting her eyes from the graffiti and sticking close to the group, she followed Evelien over to the metal staircase that led up to the exit hallway.

The staircase shuddered beneath them, unsteady after the quakes. Rusting with the passage of years. They went one at a time, white-knuckled and with gritted teeth. Metal creaked with malice until Joel took the final cautious step up to join the others. Des released a breath.

The exit sign over the door was somehow still lit; it saturated the hallway in a harsh red glow. "Everyone at once, come on," Evelien said. She placed a palm flat on the door and gripped the handle while everyone else piled around her. And they pushed.

Joel strained, shoulder against the industrial door. "It's not working," Laurel cried, leaning back.

"Shut up." Des drove her hands into it until veins were visible on her forehead.

Evelien pushed and pushed, trying to force down the unresponsive handle at the same time. Several moments passed until she shouted with exertion.

Laurel slumped to her knees, and Joel panted heavily. "Evelien, it's not going to open," Des said, standing back with hands on her head. "Let go back downstairs, and maybe we can try—"

"What—is—happening?" Evelien punctuated each word with a vicious kick to the door. It seemed to groan.

The hairs on the back of Des's neck stood on end. Joel and Laurel took steps backward. "Hey, hold on—" she reached for Evelien.

"I can't do this anymore!" Evelien took as much of a running start as she could in the narrow width of the hallway, and threw her body into the door.

Before she hit it, it opened of its own accord, and Evelien fell into a blank white void.

Evelien collapsed onto her knees into the dimensionless white and had just enough time to look back at Des with wide eyes before the heavy door shut by itself with an echoing slam.

<h1 style="text-align:center">chapter nine</h1>

DES AND JOEL POUNDED THEIR fists against the cold door. *"Evelien!"*

"Hey, can you hear us?"

"Please, Evelien—"

"Are you there?"

"Hey! Help!"

No response. Laurel muttered to herself, rocking slightly on the floor.

"Oh, god, what the fuck," Des stammered. It was as if the door had never opened at all; no scent of fresh air, no scratched markings on the floor. The handle was steadfast as ever. The strange whiteness they'd seen on the other side showed no evidence of existing, nothing able to breach the airtight hinges. The silence from the other side was nauseating.

Joel wrapped his arms around himself. "She got out. It's okay, she's out so she'll go and get help. She'll come back for us. It's fine, we just have to wait."

"Where was the alley?" Des whipped to face him.

He blinked. "…The alley?"

"The alley that leads to Redacted. Downtown Portland, off of Congress Street. The one that smells like cat piss and weed. That alley. Where was it? Did you happen to see it when the door opened? Because I sure as hell didn't." Des gave the door one final exasperated kick with a shout.

Even drenched in red light from the exit sign, Joel looked pale. "It must be daylight by now. Right? She's fine. Our eyes aren't adjusted, so everything looked bright white, but—"

"No." She felt like she was going insane. Evelien was gone. Redacted was ruined. They were cut off from reality and floating untethered into cosmic nothingness. Panic clawed its way up her throat. "No. There was no alley. There was no Portland. There was *nothing there.*" Des turned to go back downstairs to the club floor. To do what, she wasn't sure. She just needed to move.

When she reached the last of the rickety metal steps, the whole staircase wobbled and swayed. She stepped off. Joel hung onto the railing halfway up, and Laurel had followed close behind him. "Hey, one at a time!" Des yelled. Rusted bolts clattered to the floor.

The staircase gave out and fell with a ricocheting clang toward the crevasse in the floor of the basement, carrying Laurel and Joel with it.

As the metal hit the ground, Laurel was flung out to the bar on the far side of the crack. She screamed as she slumped to the floor. Joel, further down the steps, fell to the cliff's edge. The force of stairs hitting ground made him lose his grip. He clung to the dangling railing, feet swinging for traction against the exposed rocky earth.

"Shit! Hold on!" Des ran to the narrowest part of the crack and jumped to the other side. The metal staircase shifted and creaked, teetering farther into the gap. She reached Joel just as it lurched, catching on the jagged side a few feet down.

He slipped and hung with the railing under his arms. "Wait! Don't touch it," he panted before Des could grab the metal. "Too much weight. I'm gonna climb to you—"

"Then do it, now!" Bits and pieces of timeworn metal fell into the abyss and made no noise to indicate they'd reached the bottom.

Joel braced himself and inched closer. The staircase groaned in protest.

Des knelt and reached out her hand, eyes stinging.

He strained as the structure tilted dangerously. "You'll have to catch me," he struggled.

"I fucking *know*, Joel, just come on, I've got y—"

The stairs fell.

Metal clattered against the sides of the crevasse in deafening strikes. Des lunged forward and grasped Joel's arm in both of her own. It was slick with sweat; she dug her nails into his forearm and felt his weight pull and tear the muscles in her shoulders. The staircase was swallowed by the darkness and its metallic blows grew distant. The whites of Joel's eyes were visible as Des slid toward the edge, sneakers grinding into the dirt on the floor. She dug her heels in and shouted. She was going to drop him.

Laurel appeared to her right, pink hair wild and makeup running down her face. "Grab on," she extended her hand to Joel, and with great exertion, he reached up with his free arm to take it. Both girls lifted with all their strength, until Joel was able to scramble at the edge of the cliff. All three collapsed onto the flat floor, breathing heavily.

Silence as they caught their breath, staring at the sagged ceiling of Redacted. "That was gnarly," Joel finally said.

A delirious laugh bubbled in Des's chest. "Fuck. Thank you, Laurel."

She coughed. "Anytime."

The three stayed together like that for a while. Sitting on the bar side of the chasm, finding new details in the graffiti littering the place in their solemn observation. With both Evelien and Markus gone, the air felt mustier, heavier. The former's absence was particularly felt in that she'd been the only one among them who might have been sensible enough to think through a way to escape. And in a way, she had done just that.

Powerlessness was almost unbearable for Des. There was no point in pacing the vandalized remains of Redacted, no reason to search for another exit when they seemed to be stuck where the rules of time and space no longer mattered at all. It wasn't that she'd given up. She was frustrated. Wanted to rip her hair out at the roots and smash the last few dusty barstools into splinters. Like playing a game where you know you're going to lose several moves before it happens, and there's nothing you can do to save yourself. In fact, you know you're going to lose before you even start playing. You were born to lose. A rigged zero-sum game. That was what their lives had come to—working jobs they hated, to pay for apartments they couldn't afford, to get their hearts broken over and over again in pursuit of some unachievable sense of fulfillment.

So, she did the only thing she could do: she waited for another earthquake.

And that would mean they needed blood.

Joel sat with his back leaned against the bar, arms crossed and eyes shut. The alcohol had worn off by this point and all he wanted was to sleep. He might even wake up in his and Des's apartment and get to tell her about this really fucked-up dream he was having. He was teetering on the edge of consciousness when a tightening sensation shot through his lower abdomen. It was as if someone was twisting his organs in their fists. "Ah, shit." The telltale sign that he was in for a bad time.

"Huh?" Laurel looked at him quizzically from her spot against the brick wall, the cut line of the telephone sitting above her head.

He yawned. "Either of you happen to have a spare pad on you?" Joel asked.

Des blinked out of her reverie. "Pretty sure those pants are ruined either way, man," she nodded to the dirt and rips in his jeans.

"Nah, these are work pants, they can take a beating. Blood, on the other hand, would ruin them."

Laurel didn't laugh; she was staring at him. "That's not something you should joke about," she said.

His smirk faded. "Uh. I'm not joking." He scratched the nape of his neck. "Did Markus not tell you?"

"Tell me what?"

Des glanced between the two of them, absentmindedly biting a fingernail. She raised her eyebrows at him. He steeled himself. "That I'm transgender. Figured he would've told you all my secrets at this point, but whatever, guess not."

"You…are?"

"Yep." His tone was final, a challenge.

"So, Markus isn't—wasn't—queer?"

Both Des and Joel had to pause to wrap their heads around the whiplash-inducing question. "How does that relate to *anything* he just said?" Des said.

"No, I know, I just mean—it's not really the same, if you don't have a—" she gestured below the waist. "I'll admit that you were sort of right earlier. It's not a fetish, but I thought it was kinda hot, that Markus had been with another guy before. I liked it, that's all. It's why I offered, er, what I offered. I just didn't realize…I mean, it's not a problem, but—it's not the same, you know?" She tried to busy herself by fidgeting with the dangling cord of the phone.

"I don't know, actually." A muscle jumped in Joel's jaw.

Laurel seemed to shrink. "Hey, I take no issue with trans people. I'm just surprised, I guess? It changes things…"

Des ran a hand through her hair. "God, Laurel. You're digging your own grave right now."

"I'm not! I'm just saying!"

The two girls argued while Joel sighed, leaning his head back against the bar. He didn't care enough to contribute. Another cramp contorted in his lower stomach; what he'd give for another drink. Shifted in his seat on the floor. A sticky wetness made itself known in his boxers. Fuck. He'd bled through.

The dead phone rang.

Laurel and Des cut off their argument, eyes wide. The jolting receiver tone sent a shudder up Joel's spine. None spoke, and Laurel stared at the box above her head. Her fingers clutched the wire still dangling from it. Lifeless. Cut. The piercing ringing sounded again.

Des swallowed, her throat dry. "Pick it up," she said.

"What?" Laurel looked disgusted.

"Answer it." She looked to Joel, who nodded without a word.

Laurel reached for the blaring phone, which seemed to have gotten louder on the third ring. Very slowly she returned to her sitting position below the phone box, hugging her knees to her chest. Her hand was shaking as she raised the phone to her ear.

It must have been silence on the other end at first. "H-hello?" Laurel said after an eternity. Again, nothing, even as Joel and Des strained to hear anything from a few paces away.

And then the screaming began.

Laurel jumped hard with a yelp and threw the phone between them. It clattered on the floor. A cacophony that envied the shrieks of the damned emitted through the detached phone, whose wire now lay limp on the ground like a snipped umbilical cord. The noise grew as if connected to Redacted's old speakers. Two distinct voices on the other end. A man and a woman in bloodcurdling agony.

"That's Markus," Joel said over the noise, hands covering his ears.

"Evelien," Des said.

Laurel plugged her ears, knees tucked up tightly to her chest.

Des detected an ambient thunder behind those screams. It grew. Vibrated the ground until the sound was all around them and the room shook.

Joel's period. Blood was spilled.

Cracks spiderwebbed out from beneath the screaming phone, the epicenter of the third earthquake that was triggered that evening.

Des shot up on unsteady footing and lurched for Joel without a second thought. Her hand wrapped around his wrist in a vise and yanked him up to stumbling feet as the club blurred in motion around them, ground numbing their feet with the vibration. It was as if they walked upon a horrible, drunken rollercoaster, like someone had spiked their drinks. The floorboards shifted and heaved. Splintered, cracked. Rusty nails popped out of them like blisters with the violent movement.

Sobs from Laurel barely cut through the roaring of the quake as she stayed sitting under the phone box. Distantly Des recognized that Evelien and Markus's screams through the detached phone had become staticky, drawn-out well beyond what a normal lungful of breath could sustain. They howled, inhuman.

Joel braced himself on Des's arm as they rocked. "Find a safe place," he said over the din. He took a step towards Laurel and nearly brought them both down with his lost balance. The flooring separated with an earsplitting creak, a newly-formed crevasse rapidly widening between Des's feet. She gasped and leaped towards the bartop without losing hold of Joel.

The new crevasse was edged with dagger-sharp splinters of wood and nails. It shot like lightning in Laurel's direction. She looked on in a panic as the void reached her feet, clawing up the brick wall at her back before she could react. The phone box shuddered once and then fell, striking Laurel's skull with a thick, wet sound.

Her sobs stopped abruptly, face slack in an instant as tears mixed with the blood running freely from her hairline. She collapsed on the precarious floor. Blue eyes wide and glazed as her pink pigtails were slowly stained dark red.

"Fuck!" Joel screeched. Bricks tumbled out from the wall, more debris showering down in a clamor.

Des's ears rang as she agonizingly tore her gaze from Laurel's body, teetering over an advancing abyss. This earthquake was far more severe than the others. "Go, go—" she pushed Joel across the bar with no clear destination in mind, just away. Dust stung her eyes as they lost their footing on almost every step. Redacted was reduced to trembling timber and concrete. The building would buckle at any moment now. They would be crushed.

Joel and Des crawled beneath their favorite booth in the very back of the bar. Their safe place. He tucked his face into the crook of her neck and she wrapped herself around him as best she could. Breath hot and staggered as they sheltered each other from a crumbling world. The walls groaned and swayed. And they waited for the end.

chapter ten

BLINDING, ALL-ENCOMPASSING WHITENESS SENT lightning bolts of pain through Des's eye sockets and out the back of her skull. She could not see her hands in front of her face, nor feel the floor beneath her. The air was stagnant, as if nothing had stirred within it for centuries. A dull hum through her veins was the only remnant of the last earthquake.

She was still in a crouching position, that much she could tell from the aching in her muscles. Standing up would mean acknowledging more of the emptiness, taking up a physical space that she could not trust to accept her. Space that may not even exist. Des kept herself small. Realized she was no longer holding Joel. Reached out for him, arms waving and grasping for anything at all to hold on to in the white void. Breaths seemed to echo through a hollow chamber, and she opened her jaw wide to un-pop her ears. Her wrist bumped something soft and sturdy; she latched a fist onto Joel's shirt, dusty between her fingers.

"Hey—you okay? Joel? I can't see." Des wasn't sure why she was whispering.

"Des," Joel croaked, his voice turning in her direction. She felt a hand stumble down her arm and hold fast to her own. "It's so bright. What is this? Are we dead?"

She squeezed his hand. "No, I don't think so." The faintest hint of a white-hot outline came into view, as if baked into an overexposed photograph. If they weren't dead, then based on the rest of the night's events... "I think your period triggered the earthquake, and it pushed us further into the future."

Joel's chest rocked in a silent, humorless laugh.

"My eyes are adjusting, is this you?" Des's fingers brushed prickly stubble.

"AGH!" Joel lurched, and his shout echoed. "What the fuck was that?!"

"Shh, be quiet, that was me—"

"No, not your hand—"

A sound like fracturing bones came from a short distance away.

Des's stomach dropped, and the pain in her head grew sharper. Their surroundings slowly came more into focus. The whiteness remained, but now it was cut through with a series of grayish rectangular fixtures assorted into lines. Sterile and fluorescent. She rubbed her eyes and willed them to adjust. Identify anything, any possible anchor point. Hazy, warped light caught the edges of a wider, more organic shadow between two of the rectangular fixtures.

It moved, and the crunching sounded again.

Joel clutched her hand. She started at the sight of his disheveled, battered form—though she supposed she looked no better. She put a finger to her lips in a shush and hoped he could make out the gesture. Without a sound she crept along the outer limits of a hard edged fixture, pulling Joel in her wake, away from the thing crushing bone.

Except, the farther from the shadow they inched, the more similar sounds came into earshot. Like millions of hungry creatures grinding bone between their molars.

The space was a forest of the rectangular fixtures arranged into a grid, backed by white walls. And within each of these small alcoves was a creature hunched over something crackling. The beings were corpselike, bloodless, chrome.

They were people.

Des's vision finally cleared, and she slowly rose to her feet. Yes, these were people. Shoulders tensed, backs to Des and Joel, hands busy with some unseen task before them. Each being was indistinguishable from the last.

Joel opened his mouth to speak, but Des held out a hand to stop him. The muscles in her legs twitched to run but she remained frozen in place as the crunching, grinding noise continued from each of the people before them.

The room seemed to exist outside of space and time, bathed in dimensionless white from floor to ceiling and no windows to break the monochrome. If it weren't for the rows of cubicles, it would appear endless and intangible. Des backed herself into the corner of the room, and as her arm touched the rough wall, she found that it was solid brick that had been painted over with plain white.

On the far wall opposite to where they stood, a crisp corridor lead out of sight; the bathroom? And next to that, some empty shelves embedded into the wall, where bottles of alcohol would have been displayed. The skeleton of this place was familiar, but its innards were not.

"It's Redacted," Des said.

The cacophony of crackling ceased. Dozens of heads turned from their cubicles and stared at them with wide, blank eyes from every inch of what used to be the club. They had been typing at computers, large white cubes with clunky keyboards. Her heart pounded behind tense ribs, feeling exposed under their surveillance but unable to run away.

No one moved. "The exit," Joel whispered. Des looked up to where the old metal staircase used to be. Glass stairs seemed to float untethered up to a hallway where the exit door should reside. The people in cubicles stared unblinking. "Let's go."

She took a step.

They just watched.

Another.

Nothing.

She got close enough to better see one of the computers, and it had a screen of illegible written characters in a language she had never seen before. It hurt her eyes to try and read. The buttons of its keyboard were misshapen and irregular. She realized the keys were an assortment of teeth, ground down into smooth buttons that maintained their natural shape.

The person at this cubicle did not break their gaze, skin almost gray and sliced through with light blue veins. They wore a white jumpsuit not unlike prison garb, identical to that of all the others at their own cubicles.

An insane urge to apologize reached Des's lips; as if she and Joel had rudely interrupted their workday, she felt utterly misplaced, like a protuberance. Joel nudged her on and they kept walking between the rows.

This Redacted had a stuffy, humid scent. A faint hum of fluorescent lighting sounded from over their heads. Bodies packed in to cubicles that did nothing to cut through the flat atmosphere. Each workspace was coated in a thin layer of grime, dust particles sticking to corners and faded screens. As they passed, dozens of pairs of vacant eyes followed, the musty smell pervasive and overpowering. Some of the beings' veiny hands hovered over keyboards and others hung limp on their otherwise empty desks. The weight of their collective gaze was a knife trailing down her spine.

At the last row before the glass stairs, Joel stopped, taking a fistful of the back of Des's shirt. He'd gone still and fixated on the last few cubicles. The pair of them stood in stark contrast to their surroundings; dirty jumpsuits, bruises, and alcohol breath against a lifeless corporate backdrop. They were so close to the exit, enough so that Des could see a residual faint red glow of the sign at the top of the glass staircase. She gravitated towards it, but Joel remained frozen. "What is it?" Des hissed.

Joel's face lost all color apart from the dark purple bruise below his eye, dried blood from the pentagram-shaped gash almost black on his cheek. He stared at the last three cubicles in the room. Des strained to make out what had gotten his attention.

"Markus?" he said.

One of the cubicle people at the end of the row then began to type on their keyboard of teeth. The repetitive crunching sound cut through the silence. Their corpselike complexion was not the warm, rich tone that Des and Joel knew. But the eyes, the shape of their mouth. His mouth. This thing in the cubicle was Markus, and he paid no mind to either of them. The fist-sized hole in his sternum was caked in tacky, congealed black and brown blood that stained his white jumpsuit as if the wound was several hours old.

Des's throat was tight and she could not seem to get enough air.

Beside Markus was an adjacent cubicle containing a slight female frame. Des almost didn't recognize her; hair pulled back in a severe ashy knot which was a far cry from pink pigtails. That, and a jagged wound gouged down the side of her misshapen skull. Laurel pressed indecipherable keys and did not shift her half-lidded concentration from her work.

Joel stumbled over to them, choking on a sob. The noise was visceral. All of the other cubicle creatures then stood up in unison, dozens of shoes hitting linoleum in one monolithic step. They leered over their cubicles at the commotion, innumerable glazed eyes, yet they remained still. Every muscle in Des's body screamed at her to run. But Joel grasped the flimsy cubicle walls between Markus and Laurel. Neither acknowledged his presence. "Please—" he rasped.

At the very end of the row was one more person at a cubicle. Evelien, in a matching white jumpsuit, bore no visible wounds. She locked her glazed expression on Des and instead stood while her two colleagues continued typing. At the edge of her periphery Des saw every other creature simultaneously shift in their direction.

Without breaking eye contact, Evelien pulled a shard of glass from some hidden place in her desk. It may have been a bottle of cheap vodka in a past life. Its edges cut her fingers, grinding bone as she tightened her grip. Blood dripped down to the shard's tip and onto the floor. Would that cause another earthquake? Already? Des didn't think they would survive another.

"Evelien, stop!" Des strode across the floor and lurched to grab Evelien's wrist. But before she could, Evelien snatched the front of Des's shirt in an immovable fist, and raised the broken glass with its sawtooth end pointed inches from Des's face.

The room fell silent once more. She didn't dare move; staring down the bottle shard to Evelien's soulless expression, dark redness blooming between her clasped fist. Gray veins framed her temples and disappeared into her hairline, eyes locked on something in the middle distance, straight through Des as if she wasn't there at all. They were two ends of a scale precarious. "Hey, hey, it's okay," Des breathed, lifting her hands in surrender. "You're alright. Let's get out of here, yeah?" She shifted her weight and leaned as far away from the glass as she could, which wasn't far with the iron hold on her chest. One uneven breath could send the shard piercing between her eyes.

Her countenance was immobile, but Evelien parted her lips then, as if trying to form words. She blinked with the foggy distance of a dream that hadn't quite let go. A soft voice escaped with a single syllable that Des couldn't make out. "What?"

"Blood," Evelien murmured.

Des's focus darted between the glass tip and Evelien, unable to see both at the same time.

Blood. The stuff of life—consciousness and humanity distilled into one sticky substance. When Des was studying English she'd read bits and pieces from Defoe's *A Journal of the Plague Year*. Researched how it was a common medicinal practice to cut open a vein and let the blood flow, supposedly relieving the patient of any bad humors and curing them of plague. Expel that which animates your limbs in order to survive. Bloodletting. She couldn't understand how anyone, even in the time of the bubonic plague, would think this oxymoronic pseudoscience was effective. She'd even written an essay on it. Which was pretty damn good, by her standards, and probably could have influenced a new zine to print and distribute anonymously here in Redacted. The practice of bloodletting was born out of misogyny and meant to borrow a principle from an archaic understanding of menstruation, where a woman's period was their body ridding itself of hysteria (from the very organ which makes them inferior) for a short time. Nowadays, blood symbolized a death sentence for so many queer individuals. The amount of friends and acquaintances who had suddenly stopped coming to Redacted, stopped getting coffee from Des at Cracked Kettle, stopped existing without a word of explanation was staggering. Come to find out later that they'd gotten sick with it, too. It made her want to die.

Blood is life. Primordial soup. Making us who we are.

It also kills. It expunges. Letting it go may be the only way out.

But it is impossible to cure oneself of humanity.

After all, the letting of blood on this night in Redacted had preceded earthquakes, which with each iteration had further devolved the place from a niche haven to a gentrified corporate hellscape.

"We need to bleed. More. *More more more more more more more—*"

In one swift motion Evelien swiped the glass shard away from Des and below her own chin. A thick waterfall erupted from her throat. She collapsed in a gurgling heap, lips still shaping the single syllable over and over.

As her blood pooled on the white floor, the rest of the office space stirred. The macabre beings across a dozen rows of cramped cubicles shuffled, a hivemind of organisms stepping towards Des and Joel. Sounds of bones breaking, skin ripping echoed around them. Some of the creatures left severed hands behind at their desks still grasping keyboards as dark sludge sputtered out from detached wrists. Layers of meaty tissue and plain clothing stuck to chairs. The odor was unimaginable. Necrotic flesh that was suddenly disturbed, releasing a stench that stung Des's throat.

She found herself on the floor, hand resting on the side of Evelien's slack face as the groaning and frothing crowd closed in. She took the glass bottle shard from her limp hand.

Joel appeared at her side and lifted her to her feet just as the first creatures descended upon Evelien's body. They pressed disintegrating mouths to the pool of blood beneath her, making disgusting slurping sounds as they consumed the substance. Markus and Laurel were among them, dousing themselves in sickly red.

Some feral urge made her mouth salivate. In milliseconds she was able to picture the metallic taste, the warmth, and felt a flutter in her lower stomach. Something deep within Des told her to join the creatures in drinking Evelien's blood. *We need to bleed.* She wanted to swallow her whole and lose herself in the process.

A handful of the creatures rose, mouths agape and drooling red. At the forefront were Markus and Laurel. They took drunken steps towards her.

She was pushed towards the glass staircase until she tripped over the first step.

"Go, go, go," Joel said through gritted teeth. "It's not them. It can't be them."

Des choked down a sob and ascended the stairs on all fours, jolted out of near-syncope. They left smudged hand and footprints of dirt and half-dried plasma in their wake, disturbing the pristine clinical space Redacted had become. The two reached the top before the leading creatures had taken more than a step upwards; they were slow moving, but would soon overwhelm them in sheer number as an unstoppable tidal wave of decaying flesh.

Des gripped Evelien's broken bottle in her left palm as they stumbled into the blaring red light of the hallway.

The exit door would be locked, just as it always had been. As it always will be. There was no use in trying. Her fingers wrapped around the handle.

It turned.

The door swung open on corroded hinges. An earsplitting creak that cut above the bedlam of the undead ascending the staircase. The creatures seemed to slow as Des's gaze shifted upwards to take in the sight before her. Beyond the doorframe. Outside.

Joel breathed out, "…What the fuck is that?"

A membrane of tissue stretched across what would have been the opening of the door. Gelatinous with veins and sinew strewn across in semi-transparent spiderwebs, pink and pulsing and alive. No alleyway, no Congress Street, no Portland, not even the empty void that Evelien had vanished into. Nothing existed outside of Redacted besides its living organ situated snugly in the doorframe.

The bloodless undead ceased their ascent of the glass stairs; Joel could feel their starving eyes over his shoulder gazing into the maw of this thing. He found his hand ghosting around Des's wrist, where she held tightly onto a broken vodka bottle. When she turned to look at him, his heart broke into shrapnel. Tear tracks cut through the dirt plastered onto her face, black makeup smudged and running. "I—" she croaked, peering around him.

"No, don't pay attention to them," Joel said, moving to block her view of the multitude of still creatures. They seemed to be waiting for something. The glass in Des's hand was drawing blood now; it dripped down the edge of her little finger and threatened to fall. It was like a Molotov cocktail that had already been thrown; hit its target and burnt through its fuel, lying in wait and gathering dust until December was there to pick up the pieces. Even if it hurt her. A salvaged weapon from a preceding, now-irrelevant war. The membrane seemed to breathe before them.

Joel held both her hands, not caring about the blood. Waited until she could focus enough to hear him.

"Cut it," he said. "Cut us out of here."

We don't need to bleed. This place does.

The cancerous people who had come from the cubicles below surveilled them in silence. Deep in the crowd now, Markus and Laurel stood, bathed in Evelien's blood as well as their own fatal wounds. Evelien wasn't what they were truly after, though she had satiated them for a short time; they wanted something else. They were waiting.

In an adrenaline-high gesture, Des linked her bloody little finger with Joel's, a sort of horrific pinky-promise. And gave the most shit-eating grin Joel had ever seen. "That's the best idea you've had all night, baby boy."

She raised the bottle over her head on brought it down on the organ blocking the door with a cry.

It sliced open thickly. As did her hand; she screamed with the force. The undead creatures on the stairs groaned in unison as the membrane squelched and fluid flooded into the exit hallway. She cut a wider opening heedless of the pain and released more of the plasma and goo. Indistinguishable darkness peeked through the other side of the jagged folds. As fluids rushed over their shoes and down the glass staircase in steady rivulets, the creatures retreated, clumsy and disorganized, as if the discharge were noxious. The remaining membrane spasmed.

Des set her jaw, fighting against her repugnance. Reached a hand out and brushed the tissue to the side, holding the membrane open like a grotesque theatre curtain. Her eyes couldn't quite make out what lay on the other side. If she squinted, kaleidoscopic shapes not unlike the ones behind her eyelids, unfocused and undulating. Abyssal, unknown. Staring into it triggered a sense of vertigo. As if her brain was spiraling in an attempt to comprehend what lay beyond the door.

She looked back at Joel, with his abused form and swollen face under the red light. His tears had washed away a bit of the dried blood on his cheek, revealing the five points of the pentagram-shaped cut there.

She loved him so much it hurt; she would get him home. To their shitty little apartment where the heating broke last week and the landlord took days to respond to their calls. To their absurd daily routines. To good music and stupid arguments and soul-crushing zines. Where she'd come back from work smelling like coffee and burnout, both sickly sweet and horribly bitter, and he restlessly dreamed of Redacted, this third place where people like him did not have to lose a vital part of themselves in order to survive.

December waved her other hand dramatically, pointing the broken bottle into the void. Filthy, abhorrent, ridiculous. Like a court jester from hell. The look rather suited her. "After you," she said.

Joel rolled his eyes and stepped through the membranous door, wincing as it touched his skin. Des gripped the hem of his shirt as she followed close behind.

LOCAL NIGHTCLUB UNDER NEW MANAGEMENT

Late Saturday afternoon it was announced that Redacted, a controversial Portland hotspot for rock and roll nightlife, is changing ownership. The previous owners of the club were unavailable for comment, as no record of their identities has been made public.

The announcement comes amidst numerous complaints from the city for the club's patrons "inspiring anarchy and violence in the community."

When asked about the process of purchasing the club, co-owner Joel Coleridge said, "We didn't buy [Redacted]. It was given to us." There is no documentation to substantiate this point. "But it's not ours," he added. The young businessman did not elaborate further on the contradictory statement.

This developing situation is ongoing, with local real estate companies as well as out of state investors expected to make competing bids on the centrally-located commercial property now that the identities of its owners are public knowledge. The upcoming turn of the millennium and an ever-growing tourism industry in Maine are likely to make these acquisition efforts all the more common for properties across the state.

Co-owner December Paige refused to go into detail regarding her entrepreneurial goals or experience. "We just have to go on," she told our reporter. "Keep the space alive. For people like us, that's the best we can do. It's the only thing we can do. Now leave us the [****] alone."

acknowledgements

Bloodletting Go was born out of feeling disenchanted with adulthood under capitalism, miserable at an old day job, and livid with the state of the world as a whole. In case you somehow didn't gather that already.

Capitalism is like bloodletting, where an individual toils away and lets go of vital parts of themselves—creativity, passion, love—in order to survive—or earn money. In the novella, the best solution that Des and Joel can come up with to live in this lose-lose world is to take over Redacted and create their own happiness by cultivating a safe queer-owned space. It's an optimistic outlook, yes, and there are a lot of other factors that go into running a safe and sustainable space like the one those two are looking for. But the thought brings me some amount of hope. *Bloodletting Go* is at its core a cry of support for small businesses making a difference in their communities. This story helped me cope with all of these feelings, and I hope it may do the same for someone else.

Fuck AI. Fuck capitalism. Fuck fascism. ACAB. Think for yourself and make weird art.

Now, a few thank-yous are in order:

This story wouldn't exist without the influence of the filmography of David Lynch, who passed away between final drafts in spring of 2025. *Eraserhead, Twin Peaks: Fire Walk With Me,* and *Mulholland Drive* dared to be strange and hard to explain. Sometimes the most poignant stories leave their audience dazed and wondering. Searching for more. And it is a great test of authorial self-control to allow one's work to exist in that ambiguity. This novella is in many ways a tribute to that Lynchian idea; just exist, and don't give a fuck about those who don't understand. "Fix your hearts or die."

It also wouldn't exist in this self-published format if not for the film *Iron Lung* by Mark Fischbach, or "Markiplier" online.

With his directorial debut, Mark has proven that stories produced by do-it-yourself creatives can absolutely rival that of any soullessly rich mega-corporation. If that's not punk as fuck, I don't know what is.

Thank you to Katherine Silva for providing copy edits and extremely helpful feedback on an early draft. As a fellow Maine indie horror author, who also happens to be queer, I hope you know that your work is valuable and that folks like myself are looking up to you as a pillar of our genre and community.

Thank you to Evangeline Gallagher for the kickass cover artwork that perfectly encapsulates this story.

Thank you to my sibling Sully for sharing your infectious love of alternative music with me and inspiring much of this book's imagined soundtrack.

Thank you to my soon-to-be wife Celeste for your unflinching support for every project I take on, no matter how unhinged the end product ends up being.

And thank you, reader, for picking up this self-published little punk creation. Long live queer, indie horror.

DES & JOEL'S PUNKASS MIXTAPE

Gutless – Hole

Never Let Me Down Again – Depeche Mode

Waitress Hell – Heavens To Betsy

Is She Weird – Pixies

Blood One – Bikini Kill

Shining – Misfits

Jennifer's Body – Hole

Drink Before the War – Sinéad O'Connor

Ellie (E. M.) Roy (she/they) is a writer and lover of all things weird, horrific, and dark, especially when those things have a social justice bend and are rooted in a queer perspective. She has a B.A. in English from Boston University. *Let the Woods Keep Our Bodies* (2023, Ghoulish Books) is their debut novel; they are also the author of the short story "Cabin Creatures" which appears in *BOREAL: An Anthology of Taiga Horror* (2025, Strange Wilds Press). She currently resides near Portland, Maine with her fiancée Celeste, their dogs Bailey and Boo, and their cat, Maisie.

Let the Woods Keep Our Bodies
Published by Ghoulish Books, 2023
ghoulish.rip

In the small town of Eston, Maine . . . weird things happen
sometimes.

Leo Bates knows what's behind every corner in her
hometown, where she's lived her whole life. Some disjointed
memories and grief for her late parents, sure, but nothing
dangerous. Nothing unexplainable.

But the familiar becomes strange the longer you look at it.
When Tate Mulder goes missing and Leo is pinned as the prime
suspect, she can only watch as the town she thought she knew
deteriorates around her. She is forced to confront the truth about
her parents, Eston, and her relationship if she is to survive an
onslaught of conspiracies, cryptic monstrosities, and whatever is
hiding in the woods where Tate was last seen. Finding the girl she
loves may be the only way to restore balance to Eston—if such a
thing ever existed to begin with.